THE BOSS
OF ME

Seven Hardcore Erotic Stories

M.S. Thomas

FH

Contents

The Boss Of Me

It's monday morning and the summer sun is warming everything up, including me. A fire has started in me, and one that has been alight for a while. I walk into the office, looking around at all the familiar grey faces, looking for her. Her, I'm talking about my boss, Ella Baker. My married boss. I know that makes me bad, but my desire for her has been growing and growing, images of us entwined, hot and sweaty, filling my mind.

She doesn't know it yet, but I'm about to seduce her.

I see her at her desk, her slender frame inside a short blue skirt, a pinstriped shirt and black sheer tights. Her shiny black high heels finish it all off and give me a burn of warm desire between my legs. We always have a friendly chat and I try to keep calm as my eyes wander all over her lithe, fit body.

Today we have a meeting about my work, and my body burns with anticipation. She takes me down to an office at the far end of the floor. It's more private than the others. All the time we walk, me behind her, I

3

watch her body move, her perfect legs striding slowly towards the room.

She sits down at the head of the long desk, but her legs are visible as she crosses them. I burn all over, my eyes staring at those black nylon covered legs and the black shiny heels. The sun shines through the window, glistening along the curve of her leg. I ache. I'm careful not to let her see me staring.

She smiles, eyes me, and starts talking about my performance, but I can hardly concentrate on her words because my heart is booming in my ears.

She moves and suddenly her pen rolls off the desk, hits the floor. I swoop automatically to grab it. My fingers grasp it, but my eyes flick up. My heart races again, my desire igniting, a fire now raging.

She has one shoe dangling, toying with it. Then it's off, while her nylon covered toes are out in the air. My eyes fix on her red toe nails that I can just spy through the mesh of her tights. What I wouldn't give to have those toes in my mouth, my hands caressing her legs.

I straighten up, wondering how long I was actually staring at her legs.

'Thanks,' she says as I put the pen on the table. 'You OK?'

'Fine.' I smile and I can feel my face is on fire. I worry suddenly that my excitement might be obvious.

'Sorry,' she says, slipping on her shoe. 'I shouldn't be taking off my shoes at work. They were aching a little.'

'It's fine,' I say, a little too loudly. 'You can take them off.'

'Really? You don't mind?'

'No, it's fine with me.' My mind races. Before I know it, I say, 'You could probably do with a foot massage.'

4

She looks up, staring at me, looking curious and I can feel my face glowing, radiating my embarrassment. What did I just say?!

'The chance would be a fine thing,' she says, and rolls her eyes. 'My husband hates feet...'

'I love them...'

Her eyes on me again, burning through me, turning me upside down. 'Really? That's unusual in a man, isn't it? I don't think anyone would want to massage my feet, not in these tights, anyway...'

'I would.' I'm on fire. Not in a good way.

Now there's silence and she's staring at me. Am I fired?

'Sorry,' I say. 'I don't know why I...'

'You give good foot massages do you?'

I nod, my heart now racing so hard I think I might be heading for a massive heart attack.

Then she's taking off her shoe, and her foot is being extended towards me, her leg muscles tightening, her knees cutting up through the nylon. Her legs glisten as my hands reach out towards her foot. Then her foot, warm and silky is in my hands, and I'm staring down at it, my eyes fixed on her red toe nails.

So I start, hands trembling, kneeding her foot muscles, massaging her foot to the best of my abilities. I stare down at her foot, hardly able to look up into her eyes, my hands trembling as the excitement and nervousness grows. I feel the burn of excitement travelling further down, suddenly realising that I would not be able to get up straight away.

Then she lets out a little sigh as she closes her eyes, and her head falls back a little. 'Mmm...you're very good at that,' she says, opening her eyes again. 'Don't forget my ankle. Think I twisted it a little the other day.'

'OK,' I say, my voice weak. 'I move my hands up further, feeling the warmth of her foot through her tights. I start to massage her ankle and just above, which she seems to enjoy. She lets out another soft sigh, so I start to massage her calf muscle, my hands trembling even more, half expecting her to suddenly scold me for inappropriate behaviour.

Then she pulls her foot from my grasp, jerking herself away and sitting up straight, her face a little red. Had I crossed the line?

But the door to the office opened after a brief knock, and the big boss, your typical self-important arsehole, came in. I switch off from what he's saying to Ella, becoming deaf to everything around me as my fingers still tingle, my mind recalling the warmth of her foot through her tights. I wondered if she was sitting there, talking seriously to her boss, a little wet. I hoped she was and felt my trousers tighten at the prospect.

The big boss leaves at some point, and suddenly we are alone again, my heart beating so hard and fast that I think she might be able to hear it, or at least feel the vibrations. But she has changed, has withdrawn back into herself, altering the subject. Suddenly we are back on my performance, which could be better, but isn't terrible. I promise I will do better, and, just for a fleeting moment, I think I see a look in her eye, a kind of sparkle or glimmer. Then it's gone and I'm being ushered out with a polite smile.

I find myself at my desk, disorientated, my head spinning, my heart still beating, my cock a little hard. I could still feel the warmth of her feet in my hands, could picture her perfectly shaped legs.

It was over. The moment had passed. I'm deflated, and start working again, my mind hardly able to concentrate on the paper work in front of me.

The day passes slowly, every second and minute moving achingly past. Then I pack away my stuff, my eyes jumping over my cubicle to see where she was, hoping to get a glimpse of her before I left for the weekend. I couldn't see her anywhere. She certainly wasn't in her office.

'Mike.'

My head spins round. She's stood by the door I usually leave by. She walks towards me, and rests her hand, perfectly manicured with deep red painted nails.

'About what happened,' she says, looking around, seeming to make sure no one's listening. 'In my office. I don't usually...'

'I know. It's fine.'

She smiles. 'But my feet, they do ache in these shoes. I'm having some work done to my house this weekend, so I'm staying at a hotel in town. Maybe you could drop by and give me a proper foot massage.'

My breath has been sucked from my lungs. I'm unable to answer for a moment, unable to hear a clear thought through the pounding of my heart.

'Which hotel?' I manage to ask, my voice barely a grunt.

'The Continental. You know it?' She smiles, seeming to look around again to check no one's listening.

'I do. OK.'

'You'll try and pop by? Maybe tonight? I've had a long day.' She lookes down to her feet, making me follow her eyes, sweeping down slowly over her nylon covered legs and down to her shiny black heels.

I swallow, then look up to find her green eyes staring into me. She looks away.

'Maybe come by about eight?' she says.

I agree, then she is gone, leaving me to grab the rest

of my stuff and head out of the building in a daze.

My mind starts racing. She's married, I know that much. There's a ring on the appropriate finger, so where was he? She was staying in a hotel.

A hotel. It would be dark outside, with perhaps a little romantic lighting in the room. A double bed.

No, no.

Yes, there would probably be all those things, but she couldn't possibly be inviting me there for more than a foot massage, could she? My boss?

I didn't care, I decided. Whatever happened, it happened and if I got to lay my hands on her legs again, I would be happy and it would give me something to fantasise about later.

I go home, have a shower, a cold one to cool my thoughts and my desires. But it doesn't work, and the images of her start flashing in my mind, along with all the possibilities of the night ahead.

I can think of only one temporary solution to my nervousness. I get the shower gel and soap myself up, lathering my rock hard cock. I close my eyes, picturing in her office outfit, her skirt pulled up, her long legs crossed. I stroke myself, teasing my own nipples occasionally. It's not long before I'm cuming, moaning, saying her name aloud as my sperm shoots across the shower floor.

For a while I feel a little more calm. I shave, then relax, watching the clock tick away slowly.

The time passes even slower, my mind full of all kinds of sexual scenarios. I push them away, shower again, then dress in a shirt and smart trousers.

I take a cab to the hotel. I'm trembling by the time I knock on her door.

She answers and stands in the doorway, holding a glass of red wine. She's wearing a short, black, shimmering halter neck dress. Her hair is up, allowing me a view of her slightly freckled, smooth skin, her slender neck. I look down to see, with aching surprise that she is wearing polka dot black sheer tights and her shiny high heeled shoes.

She looks me over, a slight smile on her red painted lips. 'You scrub up well. Come in. Want some wine?'

'Sure, thanks,' I say and watch her cross the large hotel room that has a kind of small sitting room at the far end. The bed is large, with red and white soft looking sheets.

She pours me a glass and hands it to me. 'Shall we get started?'

I nod, taking a sip of my wine, then shakily put it down. She sits on the bed, then slips off one of her shoes, leaving it lying on the carpet as she lifts her nylon covered foot towards me. My hands shake as I touch her foot again, staring at her red painted nails. I begin to massage again, gently kneading her toes and heels. Almost instantly, she lies back a little and lets out a satisfied little sigh. I take this as a good sign, and work my way up and down her foot, hearing the nylon make a delicious noise as I massage her foot. Slowly, little by little, I move upwards, first at her heel, then her ankle. I'm soon working up and down from her calf muscle to her foot. Nothing's wrong, nothing is out of the ordinary I tell myself, as she lets out little moans, and my trousers bulge with excitement. Then I'm at her knees, my favourite part of her legs, the sharp inverted triangle shape of them pushing up into the nylon. I smooth my hands up and down her legs, my cock now throbbing with excitement, sticky with precum. My mind and eyes travel up her legs into the shadows between them, underneath her skirt, wondering if she might be a little wet.

Then she slipped off her other shoe and laid back a little, so I started working on that one, treating it to the same treatment I'd given its sibling. Again, she let out soft little moans as I worked my way up her leg. I reached her calf, her knee, then kept moving up, staring at her shapely legs through the mesh of her tights. They looked so exquisite and I longed to kiss them. My hands trembled as I began to tentatively move my hands towards her inner thigh. This would be the test, I told myself, looking up at her serene face, her slightly parted red lips, hearing the sighs of pleasure coming from her mouth.

I slipped my hand against her inner thigh, just above her knee. She gave a slight quiver, but no protest came, so I kept moving my hands, gently kneeding her muscle and flesh. Further and further up I brushed my fingers, getting closer to the warmth and mystery that lay between her legs.

I was barely three inches from that sacred place, when she sat up a little and looked at me through half closed eyes.

'What are you up to?' she asked, but not sounding annoyed, I noticed.

'Just giving you more of a massage,' I said, my voice shaking.

'OK,' she said and tilted her head back again.

I started massaging again, running my hands up and down her legs, feeling the nylon against my palms, the heat of her growing as I got closer and closer. My finger tips were now brushing the top of her thigh. My head was closer to that area now, and I swear I could smell her, the sweet honey scent of her excitement. Her moans were coming faster, a little louder.

It was now or never, so I brushed my fingers over the gusset of her tights. My heart beat even faster at the realisation that her gusset was damp. I trembled as I moved both hands up towards the gusset again, pushing her legs apart, lowering my head. I pushed her skirt up a little, and she seemed to oblige by lifting herself up. Now I could see her thighs, her bum and gusset area of her tights. There was a clear moist area between her legs. I ran my hand over that area and she let out a deep moan. I pressed a little harder, my fingers digging towards her wet opening beneath.

'What're you doing?' she asked, breathlessly, a slight smile on her face.

I didn't say anything, I couldn't as my fingers were smeared by her wetness that was oozing through her tights. I pressed firmer, rubbing my fingers over her mound, her lips, while I began to tease her clit with my thumb.

She sat forward, her eyes still half closed, a smile still on her red lips. 'You could get fired for this,' she said, but her fingers reached out and started unbuttoning my shirt, revealing my chest.

Her eyes ran all over my chest, then her hands, making me tingle all over at her touch. She smoothed her palms over my chest while I still stroked between her legs. Then her fingers found my weakness, tentatively gliding over my nipples and making them hard. I shivered at the pleasure that pulsed from my chest and down to my cock. My cock was now completely rigid, bulging against my trousers as her fingers continued to tease my erect nipples.

I reached out with my other hand, taking down her dress a little, revealing her small breasts cupped in her dark red bra. I smoothed my hand over her bra, feeling her nipple growing harder beneath it. I teased them, squeezing her breasts, feeling her get wetter and wetter. The gusset of her tights was now soaking.

11

Then there was a knock at the door.

I looked round, a little annoyed that we were being disturbed when things were just getting good. But my boss, Ella, didn't seem bothered by it at all and simply pulled down her skirt, sorted out her dress, slipped her heels back on and went to answer the door.

I sat on the bed, sipping my wine, wondering if she had ordered us room service. But then I heard voices, Ella's and another woman's. They came in, my boss and a younger woman, who had red hair, a pale pretty face. She was slender, dressed in a tight fitting green dress. She too wore sheer black tights and heels. My eyes ran all over them both as they came into the room, listening to them chat like old friends, my cock still hard, my excitement growing again.

'This is the guy I work with,' Ella said, 'Mike. Mike this is Sarah.'

Sarah smiled, looking me over, then said, 'I hear you give a great foot massage.'

I nodded, unable to speak, and watched her sit on the bed, next to Ella. Sarah slipped her shoes off, then poked out her nylon covered feet towards me. Once again trembling, I took her small foot and began massaging, working it as well as I could.

'Mmm, he is good,' Sarah said, turning to look at Ella.

Ella looked back at her, then moved her head, getting closer to Sarah's face. I felt my eyes widen as my boss's hand gently touched Sarah's cheek, bringing her closer. Then they were kissing, gently, open mouthed while I watched on, still massaging Sarah's foot. My excitement grew, my cock swelling as I watched them kiss.

Then, as I thought my excitement couldn't grow anymore, Ella lowered her hands to the straps of

Sarah's green dress. She slipped them off her pale shoulders, lowering her dress until her friend was topless. I stared at her small white breasts, her very pink nipples that were erect. Ella kissed Sarah again, but this time her hands went to her friend's breasts and started fondling them, caressing and teasing her nipples. Sarah let out satisfied little moans as she was kissed. Their kissing intensified, their tongues running along each other's lips, and necks, ears. Sarah lowered Ella's dressed, then slipped her bra lower, so the nipples of my boss were now clear for me to see. Then Sarah was lowering her head, her open mouth reaching for my boss's nipples. Her tongue darted out, running a circle round her nipple before her mouth enclosed around it she began to suck.

I could hardly take any more, so released my cock from trousers, which was now more swollen than it had ever been before. This tip of it was shiny, and wet and sticky with precum. I began to watch them, staring at their beautiful slender bodies as they kissed and caressed each other, stroking my cock. I felt as if I could cum at any moment, but I didn't want to, didn't want this moment to end.

It was at this point, I noticed my boss turn her head slightly, her eyes turning to take in what I was doing to myself. She pointed out to Sarah what I was doing. Sarah lifted her nylon encased foot and pressed it against my cock, then began to rub it up and down, stroking my cock. I let out a groan of pleasure, then I saw Ella's foot reaching out, and doing the same thing. Soon my cock was trapped between their two feet, being masturbated by their feet. I panted and moaned at the sensation of it, but then Ella's other foot found my chest and began to tease it, toying with one of my nipples, making my cock swell even more. I felt ready to explode, and Sarah must have felt it, for she began to rub my cock harder with her foot, while Ella placed both her feet on my nipples and began caressing them. The pleasure raced from my cock to my nipples, sending electricity all over my body, while my eyes stared at their naked breasts, their shapely legs. I couldn't hold back any more, and suddenly my cock was twitching and jumping like mad, and streams of warm cum started spraying over Sarah's feet and Ella's legs.

'Oh, that's more like it,' Ella said, running her tongue over her lips and letting out an excited gasp.

Sarah leaned over, poking out her tongue and licking my cum off of Ella's tights. My boss smiled, half watching me as she took hold of Sarah's foot that was now covered in my cum. She sucked her toes, cleaning her tights. Then they began to kiss again, their hands starting to explore each other's bodies as I watched on. Ella slipped her hand along Sarah's leg, caressing her thigh, getting higher until her palm and fingers were pressed against her gusset. She began to rub her hand over her clit, making Sarah let out a moan.

The sight of it all started to make me hard again, and I looked down to see my erection returning. I grabbed hold of my trembling hard cock and began to stroke it, watching them now teasing each other's clits while they kissed hungrily.

Sarah looked over to me, saw that I was excited again, then began crawling towards me, her hungry mouth opening. I leaned back as Sarah took hold of my shaft, and brought my now throbbing cock towards her mouth. She ran her pink tongue over it, up and down the whole length, then sucked the underside of my swollen erection before she began French kissing it, between gentle sucks of the tip. The pleasure raced up from my cock, electrifying my entire my body. I looked up to Ella and saw she was staring at what was happening, her hand now in her tights, fingering her own wetness. She took out her fingers then licked them, half smiling at me. Sarah had most of my cock in her mouth now, sucking, deep throating me. How could this get any better, I thought? If I could get to be inside Ella, then it would be amazing.

Ella moved, getting on all fours, heading towards Sarah's arse. I could just about make out my boss pulling down Sarah's tights, then her face getting close as she parted her butt cheeks. She was tonguing her, either her pussy or her other tight little hole. I didn't care, I was just enjoying seeing them pleasuring each other and having one of them suck me. My cock was twitching again, pleasure throbbing through me, a feeling which was intensified by the sound of Sarah moaning with pleasure as Ella expertly delved her tongue into her wetness.

Ella lifted her wet mouth from Sarah's backside, then stared at me.

'I wonder what he would like to do to us,' Ella said, a sparkle of naughtiness in her eye.

'Whatever it is,' Sarah said, taking her mouth from my cock. 'He better just do it.'

I kept my eyes on Ella, my mind flooding with dirty thoughts, of all the things I had fantasised about. I was up before I had time to think, grabbing my boss by her arm and turning her round to face the end of the bed. I took her dress off, leaving her in only her black tights. I marvelled at the sight of her beautiful, shapely arse through the mesh as I bent her over. Then I pushed my cock hard against her arse, rubbing it, forcing it between her cheeks until it was stroking her wet opening and her other tight hole. I slipped my fingers under her, finding her wet clit through her tights, and teasing it, while my cock pressed against her arse. I could hear her moan, loving my hard cock being pressed against her.

Hands slipped round me as I felt small bare breasts touching my back. Sarah's fingers found my nipples and began toying with them, getting me much harder as I rubbed my cock against my boss's arse. I pulled at her tights, tearing at the gusset until I made a hole. Her arse and wet opening were there in front of me, waiting. I licked my hand and smeared my saliva over her anus before I began pushing the tip against her, forcing my way in. She let out a deep moan as my cock started going in, trembling and twitching as I felt her arse muscles engulfing my hard cock. I throbbed as I pulled back out a little, then pushed in. The pleasure roared from my cock, right to my nipples again as Sarah teased them while she bit and sucked at my neck and ear.

'Fuck her,' she whispered close to my ear. 'Fuck her hard.'

I started to, thrusting into her arse, making Ella let out painful moans. Soon she was sighing, grunting with pleasure each time I slid out and pushed in. I put my hand under her, finding her oily wet opening, and slid a couple of fingers inside. She let out a moan of pleasure as I found the bumpy mound of her g-spot and began to massage it. She writhed as I began fucking her arse faster, harder, while my fingers went to work on her clit.

Sarah took her hands away from my nipples. I heard sounds of undressing behind me, then she appeared, completely naked in front of me. I watched her lithe, beautifully pale body walk towards Ella's head, then climb over it. She straddled her head, lowering

16

her pussy to her lips. Immediately, between moans of pleasure, Ella began to kiss and tongue Sarah's wetness. Then they were both moaning, sighing and bucking. As Sarah rode her friend's face, she reached out her hands and found Ella's breasts, her hard nipples and began to pinch and tease them.

I kept fucking Ella's tight hole, ramming my cock deep inside her.

'Swap?' Sarah asked, her eyebrows raised.

I smiled and nodded, so we swapped ends. I took my cock to Ella's mouth, and began pushing it to her lips, running it over face. Her tongue darted out, trying to taste my rock hard, twitching cock. I grasped her mouth and pushed my cock between her lips, feeling her begin to suck it hungrily. I fucked her mouth as hard and relentlessly as her arse. Her moans of pleasure were muffled by my cock. I looked up to see Sarah was now wearing a large pink strap on cock, which she slid into her friend's wet cunt. Now we were fucking my boss, from either end, spit roasting her, and she seemed to be loving it.

Sarah leaned towards me, her face reaching out to me, her mouth opening. I kissed her, still feeling Ella sucking at me like a woman possessed. With Sarah's nails finding my hard nipples once again, I couldn't take it. My cock began to spasm and I was unable to hold back anymore. I started shooting my cum into her mouth and felt her swallowing it down with a moan of pleasure.

With Sarah still ramming away at my boss's wetness, Ella started groaning, her body bucking and writhing.

'Oh God, I'm going to cum,' she almost screamed, so I went over and knelt by her groin, then tongued her clit until her juices started squirting at my face.

Ella lay there panting, breathing hard, half laughing. She got up on her elbows and looked me over.

'You give the best foot massages ever,' she said, smiling. 'I should give you a raise.'

'Let me give you regular hotel foot massages and that'll be enough for me,' I said, staring into her eyes.

'It's a deal,' she said, then looked at my cock. 'Don't suppose you're ready to go again?'

A Movie Night Surprise

Tanya answered the door dressed in a black vest top, and a short denim skirt that showed off her long tanned legs. She also wore boots. She'd straightened her blonde hair. Her cleavage was on display and she was wearing her bright red lipstick and long pink nails. She wore it all because she knew what it did to him. She was teasing him. She knew only too well that when she opened the door, his cock would twitch at the sight of her, at the thought of what they might do.

If she let him.

She'd invited him round to watch a film. Just a film, she said. Nothing else.

'You better not touch me, Simon,' she'd said, pointing her finger at him. 'We're mates. Nothing else. You best be on your best behaviour tonight!'

He'd probably got turned on when she said that, she thought. She liked to tease him sometimes. It felt nice to know she was wanted. And he wasn't bad looking. But she didn't have time for a man in her busy life.

She let him in, and as she walked she thought he might smell her, her perfume lingering behind her, and the scent of her fruity shampoo making him ache.

She sat down on the sofa, opposite her TV, crossing

her legs, letting him watch, knowing he was staring at her. She even ran a hand over her legs as she told him to sit.

'Thanks for inviting me round, Tanya,' he said.

'That's OK,' she smiled, sweetly. 'Remember, you better not try anything on...this is a couple of mates enjoying a DVD.'

He nodded. 'I promise.'

She smiled. 'You want to watch the film?'

He nodded, looking her over, seeing her tanned long legs, her lips, her cleavage. His cock must've been stirring, pressing against his jeans. She thought she could see a bulge appearing.

She pressed play on the TV and the film began.

It was the horror thriller that they'd agreed to watch. About a bunch of guys who had been paid to see how far they would go, what terrible things they'd do for money.

They watched for twenty minutes, but she was starting to find herself yawning. 'Is it me or is this film a bit rubbish?'

'Is a bit,' Simon said. 'Shall we watch something else?'

'OK, you find us something,' she said, and stood up. 'I might get a glass of wine. Want one?'

'Ok.'

She went to the kitchen, grabbed a bottle of white she'd been saving up and poured them both a glass, then took it in. When she went into the living room, she found Simon stepping away from the DVD player.

'Found something?' she asked.

'I...yeah, I brought a film myself. Want to watch it?'

'Ok.' She sat, sipping her wine, feeling curious. 'What's it about?'

'Just watch.'

The film started.

An attractive dark haired woman was alone in a big, empty house, reading. There was a knock at the door. When she answered a man was there. Good looking, rough round the edges. He'd broken down and wanted to use her phone.

She let him in, a little unsure and wary of him. He came in, looking the place over.

He said he called roadside assistance, but he hadn't.

He grabbed her from behind, and pushed her down onto the sofa. She tried to scream but he put his hand over her mouth. He started yanking up her dress, revealing her skimpy purple knickers. He tore them off as he told her to be quiet.

Then he ran a hand up between her legs as she fought to get away. He pinned her down and tied her hands together and gagged her.

He pulled up her skirt, revealing her arse, and pulled her legs apart. The camera zoomed in on her glisteningly wet opening, which he began to stroke, rubbing her clit...the woman was panting, starting to moan with pleasure...It was the beginnings of a porn film.

Simon turned to watch Tanya, noticing that she was open mouthed, rubbing one hand up and down her legs, sipping her wine too. She wasn't saying anything, just watching. She hadn't told him to turn it off. She slowly slid her hand between her legs, pulling up her skirt, rubbing herself. He imagined her knickers were already soaked with her juices. He could smell her almost, the sweet scent of her wet pussy.

He wanted to reach out and touch her, he ached for her, but he knew he wasn't allowed. It was her rule. They were just friends, nothing more.

She had one hand working her clit, one clamped

on her breast, teasing her nipple through her top, her mouth open, little pleasure filled gasps escaping her red lips.

'I want you!' Simon moaned, his cock now so hard.

She looked at him, almost severely. 'You're married! That's my new rule. You can watch! But you can't ever touch!'

'I'm so horny!' he moaned. 'I get so turned on watching you doing that!'

She smiled and licked her lips. 'You can't touch me, but doesn't mean I can't touch you!'

She moved closer, and slowly unbuttoned his shirt, revealing his bare chest. She slipped her hands inside his shirt, smoothing over his chest, but avoiding his nipples.

'Oh God!' he gasped, watching her long nails moving around his hard nipples. 'Please! Please,Tanya ! Touch them!'

'Maybe I will.'

Her hands caressed his shoulders, his neck, his stomach, brushing close to his nipples. He panted, groaning, begging her to touch them.

Then her palms brushed over his nipples and the pleasure tore through him, going straight to his erection, swelling his cock even more.

She put her leg over his lap and he stared at it, the tanned, glistening shape of her thighs as she teased his nipples.

He reached for his cock, but Tanya held up a finger.

'No! You're not allowed to touch your cock, not unless I say so.' He felt his cock twitch and throb at her touch, but he kept his trembling hands at his side.

Then suddenly she pulled her hands from his shirt and went back to touching herself, stroking her clit and her wet lips. She got up a little while later and came back with her large vibrator and turned it on.

She began teasing her clit as he watched helplessly, his cock aching for her. He was opened mouth as she pulled up her skirt, revealing that she had no underwear on. She pulled her skirt right up so she could reach her wet opening, and began inserting it into her opening that was now incredibly wet and glistening.

'You can touch yourself now,' she said, and he scrambled to release his rock hard cock.

It shot out, red and purple and shiny, soaked with pre-cum. He gripped it and stroked it, watching her pleasuring herself and moaning. She was pushing her vibe deep inside her, in and out, fucking herself so hard. Then she moved, bent over the couch and reached the vibe round to her tighter hole and started teasing it as she fingered her clit.

He could now see both holes and it was more than he could take. He grabbed her arse, bit his fingers into it. She swung round, glared at hm.

'I said no!' she shouted. 'You're not allowed to touch!'

'I have to!'

'No! You don't!' She tried to pull her arse away from his grip, but he grasped her tighter. Then he pushed her face down into the sofa, weighing her down. He pulled up her skirt, staring at her delicious arse. He spread her cheeks apart, so he could slip his hand under her, cupping her juicy wetness.

'No Simon!' she scolded, trying to pull herself away.

'Stop moving!' he said. Then he ran his hand up and down her juicy pussy, feeling her oily wetness coating his hand. He licked her juices off his fingers, then went back to caressing her clit, using his thumb to tease her tight little anus. She gave a gasp and moan every time he stroked her, but kept saying, 'I haven't said you're allowed.'

'You like it. That's why you're so wet,' he said and put his mouth over her arse, and ran his tongue over her tight little hole as he teased her clit. She was getting wetter, even though she was telling him to behave between moans of pleasure.

'I haven't given permission yet,' she said, but his cock was hard and full of blood as he took it out, still staring at her wetness.

He pushed his rock hard cock between her arse cheeks. She tried to clamp herself shut, but he kept running his cock up and down her crack. He kept fingering her wet opening, pushing two fingers, then three inside. She moaned, but kept saying no. She tried to push him away, but weakly, so he kept stroking her pussy and clit.

'You're so wet, you're loving it,' he said.

He pushed her arse into the air, then pressed his cock against her soaking wet opening. He pushed hard into her vulva, getting as deep as he could.

'You're so wet,' he groaned as he pulled out a little, then shoved his cock deeper into her. She was so wet. Then he teased her tight little hole, slipping a finger into her, making her moan and plead for him to stop. Then he put two fingers and then three into her arse as he kept fucking her pussy, harder and harder.

Then he slipped his cock out of her wetness, and used her juices to coat her tight hole. He pushed the tip of his cock to her anus, making her cry out. Then he forced his way in, pushing deep into her, and hearing her let out a deep sigh. He began to fuck her slowly in her arse, as he finger fucked her pussy. He put four fingers in her as he fucked her tight little hole. He almost came, it felt so good fucking her tight arse. But he held back as he grabbed her hair and yanked it hard, making her groan and sigh with pleasure. She liked the rough stuff, had fantasised about all this kind of thing, she had told him before.

He got up and pulled her off the couch.

'On your knees,' he gasped.

She did as she was told and looked up at him.

He was still rock hard. 'Suck my cock. I know you want to.'

'It's wrong. I can't.'

She hesitated, so he pushed his twitching throbbing cock to her red full lips, rubbing it all over her face until she started lapping at it, licking it up and down. She took the tip into her hungry warm mouth and began sucking it. He began to ram it into her throat, getting harder as he heard her cough and choke. He kept pulling out, then ramming it into her mouth, grabbing her hair and forcing her head to take his full length deep into her throat. All through it, he could hear her moans of pleasure and knew her pussy would now be dripping wet.

It was time for his surprise. He took out his mobile and dialled a number. When the call was answered, he said, 'We're ready for you.'

He could see the confusion on Tanya's face when a few minutes later the doorbell rang.

He went and answered it and brought a blond man into the room. She recognised him as Jay from their office. He was not bad looking, lean but quite muscular. He was wearing a tight T-shirt.

'You know Jay,' Simon said, smiling as he saw the shock and confusion on Tanya's face.

'What?' Tanya said. 'What's going on?'

'Jay, why don't you lie down on the sofa,' Simon said, and Jay smiled, then did as he was asked.

'Tanya,' Simon said, 'Why don't you take Jay's trousers and boxers off for him?'

She knelt down and slowly, nervously began to pull Jay's jeans and boxers down. She took them off and put them on the floor. Jay was getting hard, but he grabbed his thick, tanned cock and began stroking it, getting it so much harder, and making it drip with precum.

'Tanya,' Simon said. 'I know you want to suck his cock, so why don't you?'

'I can't do that!' she said.

'Yes you can.' Simon slapped Tanya's arse a little.

Immediately she began to taste Jay's cock, running her tongue up and down the shaft.

'Taste's good, does it?' Simon asked. 'Keep tasting, tease him, suck his cock.'

Tanya did as she was ordered, using her tongue to tease his now incredibly hard cock. Jay began to moan, leaning back, removing his T-shirt, and running his hands over his own chest. Tanya kept licking away, sucking, watching Jay's face as he moaned and seemed to enjoy himself.

'Does he taste good?' Simon asked.

Tanya nodded, noticing that Simon was now sat on the sofa watching, stroking his hard, swollen cock. She became wet as he watched her sucking another man's cock. She was loving it.

'Talk to me,' Simon said.

Tanya stopped licking. 'He tastes good.'

Then she went back to licking and sucking Jay's cock, intent on making both of them want to cum, knowing she had the real power. This was her fantasy.

Watching it all, Simon was throbbing, so hard. He took himself out and sat next to Jay watching them both, stroking his own cock while Tanya sucked it.

Tanya was lapping away, tasting Jay's cock, now moaning herself with pleasure, enjoying making a man want to cum in her mouth.

Simon saw that Tanya was watching him too, watching him stroking his length, watching the precum dripping from the tip. Simon grabbed Tanya's hair, yanked her mouth away from Jay's cock and shoved his cock to her lips, rubbing it over her face as he stroked himself.

He started to cum, shooting cum at her face, splashing it over Tanya's lips. She hungrily, moaning with pleasure, licked the cum from her lips and his throbbing cock.

'Which tastes better?' Simon asked. 'My cock or Jay's cock?'

'Your cock.' Tanya smiled and licked her lips.

'Good answer,' Simon said. 'Keep sucking his cock.'

Tanya went back to tonguing and sucking Jay's cock, then started fingering his tight hole too, making him start to orgasm.

Simon walked round behind Tanya and grabbed her arse, and pushed his rock hard, twitching cock back into her tight arse, filling her up, making her cry out with pain and pleasure. As he rammed his cock deep into her arse, Tanya took Jay's cock deep into her throat, feeling him throb, ready to cum.

Simon had other ideas. 'Turn round. Suck my cock!'

Tanya crawled round and obediently began to hungrily feed on his juicy, solid cock, while Jay got on all fours and crawled behind Tanya and spread her arse apart and began lapping at her clit and pushing his fingers into her anus. Tanya began to moan and sigh and pant as she sucked and licked Simon's cock. 'Oh fuck,' she cried as she started to cum as Jay expertly tongue-fucked her arse and pussy.

Simon couldn't hold out much longer and started to throb and twitch, filling Tanya's mouth and throat with his warm cum.

They all collapsed to the floor and lay there panting like animals, all feeling dirty.

'How was that?' Simon asked Tanya .

'I've never cum so hard,' she said, still panting.

'Just wait and see,' he said and gave a wolfish smile. 'Lie on your side on the sofa.'

She looked suspicious, but did as he requested, waiting. Simon and Jay both joined her, both hard, both smiling.

First Simon slipped his hard, throbbing cock into her pussy, which was so wet, then Jay pushed his cock into her tighter hole. She gave a cry, feeling both of them, so hard, filling her up. She felt like she might burst. She could feel both of their stiff, blood filled cocks pumping, making her moan, pant and want more of it. 'Oh fuck me!' She moaned. 'Harder!'

They did, pounding both her holes until she felt Jay's cock twitch deep in her arse, and suddenly she was flooded with his cum, filling her up, and dripping down her legs. Simon was still fucking her, moaning himself, pushing deep into her. Then there were bursts of electricity over her skin, making her orgasm begin and rise up through her. She moaned as she started cuming: 'Oh fuck me, Simon, Oh shit..shit I'm cuming.'

He didn't cum, just pulled out along with Jay, who started putting his clothes on.

'I've got to go,' Jay said. 'It's been fun. Thanks.'

When the front door shut, Simon looked down at her, his cock still hard, and shiny and wet with her juices. She felt used, and Jay's cum was still deep inside her. She was still incredibly horny, but this was all so wrong.

'We shouldn't have done this,' she said, 'We're bad people.'

'No one has to know but us,' he said, smiling as he laid on the sofa.

She was incredibly horny. She huffed, but smiled as she crawled towards him, taking the rest of her clothes off, straddling him.

'As long as no one ever knows,' she said, getting on top of him, grabbing his still hard cock and slipping it inside her. It felt great, sliding down on him. She was so wet.

She sat up, looking down at him, watching him groan as he looked up at her. She reached out her hands, began teasing his nipples with her nails, feeling him grow even harder inside her. She began to ride him hard, feeling his cock twitch. She was going to cum again, and she wanted him to as well. She toyed with his nipples, riding him hard, pushing her pussy down on him. He moaned, thrusting his cock deeper up into her as she bucked down on him.

'Oh fuck, I'm going to cum, Simon,' she moaned, looking down at him.

'I'm cuming!' he cried, then she felt him twitch and his cum spurting inside as her orgasm came. She fell down onto him and looked him in the eyes. 'That was fucking great, but nobody better find out about this!'

'No one ever will. Our secret,' he said and laid back.

THE LIFT

Andy was daydreaming, feeling bored, watching the people in his office go by. It was the same old thing, day after day, and there wasn't much to keep him occupied. He stared at his computer screen, deciding he really should be doing some work. But then he looked up when he saw HER walking by his desk, striding across the office, carrying her flask of coffee. He'd got to know Julie, befriend her, enter her world. But he had a secret sexual crush on her. She was wearing the jeans, the pair of jeans that were his favourite. The dark blue ones that looked as if they'd been spray painted on her body. She wore a tight beige jumper that clung to the shape of her nice sized breasts. Her straight blonde hair, her big dark brown eyes, it all made him stare at her.

She disappeared again, going off somewhere, so he was left with his work. Then he looked up, realised it was his break time. He had some food, but he didn't really feel hungry.

He was too horny to feel hungry. Then he had an idea, and he couldn't resist the urge. He hurried through the corridor, heading downstairs, making sure no one was around, then slipped into the toilets. He went into a cubicle and shut the door.

The downstairs toilets were hardly ever used so he knew he wouldn't be disturbed.

He quickly took out his mobile phone, and brought up Julie's Facebook account, then found his favourite photographs of her, profile shots where she'd been going out somewhere. She looked hot, all dressed up, her make up on.

He balanced the phone on the window ledge in the cubicle, then unbuttoned his jeans, slipped out his cock that was already getting stiff at the sight of her photographs. It helped him imagine a scenario in his head, a moment when something might happen between them. It was unlikely, but he liked to fantasise as he gripped his now rock hard cock, and stroked it. He imagined she might have given him a lift home, and taken him up on his invite to come in for a quick coffee. His cock got even harder, precum shining on the tip as he imagined maybe trying it on. She would go with it, kissing him back, his hand slipping into her knickers, feeling that she was gushing with juices already...

Then the door to the toilet opened- somebody had come in. Shit. The spell was broken, so he stood there, waiting for his erection to go down so he could head back to work.

He spent the next hour disappointed, feeling horny and remembering he had an appointment at a hotel out on Dartmoor. It was a job interview, but he had no idea how to get there and was going to order a cab.

He went to the cafe on the next floor for his next break, bought a coffee, and sat there, staring into space, worrying about what the interview would entail.

'What you doing after work?' a familiar female

voice said behind him.

He turned round to see Julie sitting behind him at a table, drinking a tea, sat next to a mutual friend called Dave.

'Er...I've got a job interview,' Andy said.

'Don't say that too loudly,' Dave said, laughing.

'Where?' Julie asked.

'Some hotel on Dartmoor. Not sure really.'

'I can give you a lift,' Julie said.

Andy shook his head, even though already his mind flashed with all the arousing possibilities. 'Don't worry. I'll get a cab.'

'You're not getting a cab. That'll cost a fortune! I'll drive you. I haven't got much to after work, I don't pick up my son until later from his dad's. It'll be an adventure.'

The thought of being in a car with her, after the things he'd been fantasising about, made him a little nervous. But also a little excited. 'OK. Thanks. That'll be great.'

She got up, finishing her coffee. 'Good. I'll meet you in the car park after work. Mine's the red Peugeot.'

'All right, I'll meet you there.'

He watched her go, his eyes falling all over her, especially her bum as she moved, swinging side to side. He ached and his cock twitched.

Later on, when work was over, Andy headed down to the car park and found Julie already sitting in her car texting. She was so engrossed in her phone that when he knocked on the window of her car, she almost jumped out of her skin.

'You scared the crap out of me,' she said and put away her phone.

'Sorry,' Andy said, climbing in beside her.

'It's Ok. I was just texting my baby sitter. Right, let's go.'

Andy looked over at her as she drove them away from the car park, noticing with widening eyes that she had changed out of her jeans into a short denim skirt, so he could now see her shapely legs. His cock throbbed a little at the sight of her sitting next to him as she drove out of town and across the moors.

They made idle chit chat on the way, discussing work and people they liked and didn't. Soon they seemed to be deep on Dartmoor. Julie had said she knew the way to the hotel, but suddenly she pulled up at a junction in the middle of nowhere, looking a bit confused.

'I could've sworn it was this way,' she said, looking both ways. 'But now I can't see any signs for it. Sorry, I'm getting us lost.'

'It's Ok. Maybe if we keep going along this road, we'll see it.'

'We'll see,' she said, putting her car into gear.

Andy thought he heard it make a rumbling sound as they headed up the narrow lane. Then the car totally conked out, coughing and spluttering.

'Shit,' Julie said, the car rumbling, about to give out. 'Oh no. What shall I do?'

Andy looked ahead and saw a turning for a car park. 'Pull into that car park just up ahead.'

Julie steered it while there was still a bit of life in it, managing to enter the small car park that had only a few empty cars in it. She pulled up just as the engine coughed and gave out.

'Shit,' she moaned and turned the ignition key, but the car hardly made a sound. 'It's dead. Shit. I better call the RAC. Sorry, don't think I'm going to get you to your hotel.'

'It doesn't matter. Let's just get your car fixed.'

She smiled, then searched in her glovebox for her card, then got out, and made the call. As she talked, she walked round the car. Andy watched her, feeling the build up in him, the desire burning all over. His cock was warm, getting a little hard. They were stuck in the middle of nowhere together. It was kind of cosy.

When she climbed back in, she sighed and sat back. 'Well, they said it might take an hour to get here. Sorry about your interview.'

'Don't worry. I didn't really fancy working in a hotel anyway.'

She smiled. 'What're we going to do for an hour?'

He could think of a few things he'd like to do. 'I don't know. Play ISpy?'

She laughed. 'Think we can come up something more fun than that. What about...truth or dare?'

'Er...ok...'

'I'll pick a truth for you...'

Andy's heart started to beat in his chest. 'Right...'

She sat there staring out the window, thinking. 'Is there anyone you fancy at work?'

'Er...'

'Come on, you can tell me...'

He could feel himself going red. 'Maybe...'

She looked at him slyly. 'I thought so. I won't ask who...yet. Your go.'

'Hmm...' his mind whizzed. 'Truth.'

'OK?'

'You ever been married?'

'No. That's a rubbish one. You can do better.'

'OK.'

'Try harder.'

'OK. His heart beat so fast. 'Ever come to work

without knickers on?'

She laughed, But tried to looked shocked. 'Andy! How dare you! Ha ha. Maybe. A couple of times. Don't tell anyone! My turn!'

'Go on.'

She seemed to think. 'Dare! I dare you to go outside, then flash your bum!'

'What?! No way!'

'There's no one around!'

'You're here!'

'I know. Go on! Don't be chicken!'

He shook his head. Then he climbed out, heading across the car park, looking around for anyone. He looked back at Julie in the car and saw her egging him on.

He looked around again, then quickly undid his belt, pulled down his trousers and flashed his bum. Then he hurried back to the car and climbed in, his face warm from embarrassment.

'That was a bit quick!' she said. 'I didn't think you could move that fast! My turn!'

'Ok. Truth or dare?'

She smiled. 'You pick.'

He smiled, then looked out the window. There was no one around...apart from him. 'Go outside and flash me...'

She laughed. 'Flash what?'

'Your...bum!'

She shook her head, then started to get out. 'Too easy.'

Then he watched her walk to the front of the car, adjusting her skirt, lifting it up, revealing her red thong and her nice shapely bum. She pulled her skirt down again as he felt a twitch in his trousers.

She climbed in again and shut the door. 'There you

go!' she said, grinning. 'Dare done. Now I get to dare you!'

'OK...' now he wasn't feeling so brave as he saw the mischievous glint in her eye.

'Hmm...' she said, pretending to scratch her chin. 'I think I'll dare you to...go outside and flash your, you know!'

'What?! No way! My...my thing?'

'Go on! Go out there and get it out...but...'

He tensed up.

'It has to be standing to attention!' she said, raising her eyebrows.

He stared outside, trying to see if anyone was around. 'You're joking?'

'Nope. Don't be chicken. Go on, hurry up!'

He looked around. 'It has to be...?'

'Yes!'

He climbed out, then walked to the front of the car, still keeping an eye out for dog walkers or hikers. There didn't seem to be anyone around. But she said it had to be standing to attention. How was he going to get hard?

He unbuttoned himself a little, then slipped his hand into his trousers, finding his cock, and giving it a stroke. He was feeling nervous and he wasn't getting very hard. Then he looked round and saw Julie watching him, smiling, egging him on.

The sight of her automatically made him get hard, so he lowered his trousers and his boxers and let his cock spring out, all hard and a little bit wet with precum. He stroked it a bit, quickly, while looking at her, then pulled his trousers back up and ran back to the car.

'Well done!' she said, clapping. 'I'm impressed.'

He blushed, wondering what exactly she was

impressed by. He knew exactly what he was going to dare her to do next. Flash her breasts. He'd seen them under her tight tops, and he was dying to see them for real.

'Ok, I choose...' she began to say, but then a car pulled into the car park. It was a dark blue Peugeot estate car, with a man and woman at the wheel. They parked a hundred yards away, almost parallel with Julie's car.

'Talk about spoil our fun,' Julie said.

He was disappointed too. Just when he was going to get to see her breasts. Maybe more.

The woman and man stayed there, just sitting, looking out at the view. They seemed to be in their mid thirties. The woman had dark hair, and looked quite pretty from where he was. The man had short brown hair, looked in shape. But every now and again, they kept looking over at Andy and Julie.

'What do you think they're up to?' Julie said.

'No idea,' Andy said. 'But they keep looking at us.'
'Weird.'

Andy saw the young woman taking off her seat belt, then seemed to be take off her coat. Then her top.

'Is she?' Julie started saying.

And yes, as Andy kept watching, the woman took off her top, and sat there in a black and red lacy bra. Her breasts were quite big, and her cleavage was extremely attractive in her bra.

Then the man took off his top, revealing a chiselled, tattooed body. They started to kiss, hungrily, touching each other.

'Is this really happening?' Julie asked.
'I think it is.'
'Have we accidentally come dogging?' 'Yes, we have.'

'Let's keep watching.'

'Ok,' Andy said, a little flustered but aroused.

The fact that he was sat next Julie and they were watching hot people getting off, was making Andy grow hard again. He tried to hide his erection as the woman's head suddenly lowered, her mouth opening. The man leaned back in his seat, his face twisting into a pleasure filled expression. Yes, she was sucking him off. From where he was, Andy could see not only her head bobbing, but her cleavage. His cock twitched again.

Eventually the couple moved, stripping off the rest of their clothes, moving the seats back, getting into a doggy position. The man was hard, his big cock getting ready to plunge into the woman's pussy. He grabbed her arse, and pushed himself deep inside her, fucking her hard, ramming into her, slapping her arse every now and again.

Andy was getting harder. He looked over at Julie and saw she was just as hypnotised by it all. The couple obviously loved being watched.

Soon the couple stopped, and the man pulled on some clothes while the woman sat, naked in the car playing on her phone.

The man started to walk over.

'He's bloody well coming over!' Julie said, blushing.

He knocked on the window, so Julie lowered it.

'So, you two like what you've seen so far?' he asked, looking them both over.

'Er, yes...' Julie said. 'Very...sexy.'

'I can see he's enjoying it,' the man said, his eyes looking at the bulge in Andy's trousers. Julie looked down too, her eyebrows rising.

'You can get it out, mate,' the man said. 'We're all friends here.'

Julie looked at Andy, a smirk on her face. 'Go on, Andy, you heard him. Get it out.'

'Er...'

Then Julie grabbed his flies and undid his trousers and helped him get his now very hard cock out.

'That's better,' the man said. 'Want to see us do some more?'

'Er...yes,' Julie said.

'Good. Cause I've got a mate turning up in a min,' the man said, then patted the car then walked off.

'What do we do?' Andy asked.

Julie shrugged. 'Well, haven't got much choice. We can't go anywhere yet. Might as well enjoy the show.'

Another car turned up with a man in it. He parked up, then got out and headed to the car with the couple in it.

'He's pretty fit too,' Julie said.

Andy didn't say anything just watched as they all climbed in the back, getting the woman between them. The men got themselves hard, stroking their cocks, then grabbed her. Her boyfriend grabbed her arse, then pushed his cock deep into her pussy, fucking her hard, while his friend got his cock and grabbed her by the hair. He pushed his cock into her mouth, and she began to lick and suck like her life depended on it. She was being fucked from either end, spit roasted and she seemed to be loving it. The men were both quite muscular with tattoos round their arms and their muscle flexed as they rammed into her, fucking her completely. They had the windows open and the girls muffled pants and moans were loud enough for Andy and Julie to hear.

Andy felt his cock getting harder, then looked down and saw that it certainly was rock hard. Then he turned and caught sight of Julie. She had slipped her hand into her jeans and was rubbing between her legs. Andy got even harder, his eyes jumping between her and the sex car.

The two men changed position, getting the girls arse in front of them, spreading her legs. One got his cock into her arse, the other into her pussy. They started fucking her, pounding her hard, making her practically scream out.

Julie was stroking between her legs, watching. Andy slowly took hold of his cock, grasping it and slowly began to stroke himself, half watching the car, half watching Julie. He imagined she was soaking wet and he so wanted to feel it.

But he kept on stroking his cock, feeling himself twitch with excitement.

Soon the guys stopped fucking her, and she repositioned herself, sort of to the side. Andy wondered what was going to happen. Then he realised as the newly arrived friend lowered his head and put his mouth round his friend's big juicy cock. He started licking and sucking his friend, obviously sending his mate into a state of ecstasy, while the girl then got herself under the friend and started sucking him. Andy looked at Julie as she let out a sigh, her hand now working her pussy hard. She was obviously getting aroused by it all. Andy started stroking his cock, watching Julie, feeling himself wanting to cum. But really he wanted to cum inside her more than anything.

After a little while the man was coming across to them again, now with his clothes on. He leaned in the window.

'Right, time for you two to return the favour,' he said.

'Excuse me?' Julie said. 'What do you mean?'

'Tit for tat,' he said, winking. 'We want to watch you two go at it. Alls fair and all that.'

Julie looked at Andy. She raised her eyebrows. 'I guess...OK.'

The man nodded, then went back to his car, joining the others as they sat waiting for a performance.

'What are we going to do?' Andy asked.

'What else can we go?' Julie said. 'We're stuck here and we kind of owe them!'

Andy was thinking that this was a bit of luck. But he hadn't planned to do anything with Julie in front of an audience.

'Here we go,' Julie said, taking off her top, then slipping off her skirt. Suddenly she was in her red thong and matching bra, showing off her tanned body. She looked great and Andy became immediately very hard again.

The next thing he knew, Julie was leaning towards his cock, her full lips opening. Then he felt her warm mouth enclose the tip of his cock as her hand grabbed the shaft. She began to suck him, her head bobbing, her tongue licking his cock, making a pulse of pure pleasure race through him. Julie was sucking his cock, and three people were watching. When he looked over to the car, he saw the two men watching. The woman was in between them, her arms moving, her hands obviously gripping both their throbbing cocks. They obviously liked what they saw.

Andy looked down and felt like he wanted to cum as he saw and felt Julie hungrily sucking him off. Then he heard her moan and realised one her hands was still in her thong, teasing her wet pussy. She was loving it and must have been so wet.

She took her mouth away from his cock. 'Are they watching?' she asked, panting.

'Yeah,' he managed to say, then put his hand on her head and pushed her back towards his awaiting, hard cock.

Her mouth started sucking again, then he looked down at her lovely arse and the red thread of fabric that separated her arse cheeks. He couldn't resist and ran his hand down to her arse and squeezed, making her let out a moan as she licked him. Then he ran his hand down further, under her arse, and found the gusset of her thong, which was soaking wet. He felt the warmth of her, as he let his fingers move it aside, finding her juicy wet pussy, then her clit. He stroked it, making her suck him harder, teasing the little wet and hard bud. She loved it, hungrily sucking him as he teased her. He decided to use his thumb, daring to tease her little tight hole with it. Her ran his thumb over her hole, feeling her buck and moan and suck him with even more hunger.

'We better change positions,' she said. 'They'd expect it.'

He nodded as she got on the seat, getting her arse in the air. He pulled her arse close to him, then pushed his cock deep into her wet, now warm pussy. He slid in, making her let out a loud groan of pleasure. Her head lifted, watching the car opposite and the men who were being wanked off by the woman between them.

She started to moan louder, obviously being turned on by the fact that she was being watched. Andy rammed his cock deeper into her pussy, feeling how wet she was getting. She was gushing with juices. He slipped one hand under her and began teasing her clit, which had the effect of making her groan even louder. Then he parted her arse cheeks so he could see her little puckered tight hole. He moved his hands along her soaked pussy and wiped them over her tight little hole. She bucked a little, moaning harder as he ran a finger over the puckered hole. Then he pushed a finger into it, feeling the juices lubricating the hole, letting him sink a finger inside. Then he put another, then another, until he had three fingers in her arse, and his cock ramming her pussy. Now she was groaning and moaning hard, her face towards the other car.

'Oh fuck...' she moaned as he slid his cock out of her and left the tip inside. Then he pushed deep into her again, while putting a fourth finger into her puckered whole, stretching her wide. Then he decided to swap over, sliding his cock out of her pussy and pushing it into her tight hole. She let out a loud pant and moan as he started to fuck her arse hard. She was tight and it made him want to shoot his load right deep inside her dirty hole. He used his fingers to finger fuck her pussy, an action that made her shout, 'Oh...shit...that's it, fuck me...harder...finger my pussy.'

He kept on fucking her tight hole, loving every moment, hardly believing he was getting to carry out his fantasy.

'What...what...are they doing?' Julie said.

Andy looked up to see the two men, now partly dressed, but their hard cocks bulging in their trousers, coming towards Julie's car.

The friend leaned in. 'Nice work. You're getting us really hard. How about we swap?'

'What?' Julie said.

But the friend had the door open and was helping her out of the car, before she could protest. Andy watched on, feeling a bit wary, and seeing that Julie was unsure herself.

'Come on,' the man and the friend said, practically carrying her back towards their car.

But Julie stopped them. 'I don't know about this...'

'Really?' the friend said, then slipped his hand between her legs, cupping her. 'You're very wet...'

'I don't think I should...' Julie said.

But the friend kept teasing between her legs as Julie tried to remove his hand. But the man put his arms round her, slipping down her bra and cupping her breasts and teasing her nipples.

'Are you sure?' the man asked. 'I'll stop if you say so. Just have to say.'

She opened her mouth, but only a pant came out.

'Yeah, changing your mind?' the friend asked, taking down her knickers and fingering her pussy. She tried to remove their hands as she said, 'I'm not sure...'

But the friend kept fingering her pussy, teasing her, saying, 'I bet you'd like both our big cocks inside you...wouldn't you?'

'I don't know about...' she said.

'Go on...say it...tell us you want both our cocks inside you.' The friend kept teasing her pussy. Andy could hear, almost frozen In his seat, Julie, moaning a little as she was being teased. He'd hardly noticed that the woman from the other car was coming over and climbed in beside him. She only had her bra and knickers on as she sat and smiled at him.

Andy smiled back, but kept watching what was happening with Julie, wondering if she needed rescuing or not. But she was moaning, even though she was staying, 'You'd better stop...'

But the men kept touching her, stroking between her legs, teasing her nipples.

'Say it,' the friend said, his hand pressing to her pussy, perhaps even fingers sliding in, Andy thought. 'Say you want us both to fuck you, both our cocks inside you...'

'Oh...shit...you'd better...' Julie was saying, panting.

Then Andy was stunned as Julie suddenly said, groaning, 'Oh...shit...fuck me...I want your cocks inside me...'

He felt jealous, but why did his cock, that was still on show, get so hard? He looked down. His cock was solid and glistening with precum.

They got Julie on the front of the car, not inside this time. They laid her across the bonnet, a man at either end. The main man grabbed her from behind and pushed his thick cock deep inside her pussy. The friend pushed his cock at her mouth, rubbing it over her full lips. Then he forced her mouth open and started to ram his cock into her mouth while his mate started to fuck her pussy. Andy could only watch while the woman he'd just fucked, was being fucked by two strange men. Andy felt something and looked down to see the woman had hold of his hard solid cock and was stroking it. He looked at her, saw she was smiling, and that her cleavage was on display.

She took his his free hand and guided it to her knickers and slipped it inside. She was very very wet. He started teasing her, caressing her, oiling her pussy lips with her juices as she pulled his cock, stroked it. He found her clit and teased it, making her moan. But his eyes turned towards Julie as he was still being fucked by the two muscular, tattooed men. She was moaning as she was fucked hard from both ends. They were hammering her hard and fast. And she was loving it, moaning louder and louder. Andy was getting harder.

Suddenly the woman lent over him, taking his cock into her mouth. She kissed, licked and sucked it. She obviously loved sucking cock because she was moaning as she did it.

Andy looked up, now filled with pleasure, his

cock throbbing and twitching in her mouth. The two men moved Julie, bent her over the bonnet of the car and pushed both their cocks into her. The main man pushed his cock in Julie's pussy, the other into her tight hole. Andy watched as they started fucking her, and he could hear Julie gasping and moaning as they hammered her, ramming their cocks deep into her. He looked down and saw the woman sucking his cock.

She stopped and said, 'I want you to fuck my arse.'

Then Andy watched her as she climbed in the back after removing her knickers. She got herself in a doggy position, so Andy joined her and used her juices to lubricate her tight hole. He pushed his cock in, finding her tight hole very welcoming as she started to moan.

'Oh yes, fuck my dirty little hole,' she moaned, and he did, pushing his cock deep into her, his eyes turning towards Julie who had two cocks inside her and was being completely used. The sight of Julie being fucked like crazy made him want to cum and his cock started to throb and twitch.

'Oh yes, fill me with your hot cum,' the woman said, so Andy let go and began to spurt his cum deep inside her. He panted after he'd cum, worn out, a little sad that he hadn't cum inside Julie. 'Thanks for that,' the woman said, as she straightened herself out.

But Andy's attention was back on Julie and the two men that were still fucking her hard. He stepped out of the car, getting closer to the scene, hearing Julie now moan and groan in time with their thrusts.

'I'm...oh fuck...' she shouted, 'I'm going to cum!'

So they fucked her harder, until she let out a shout and cry. It was obvious she was cuming but they didn't stop.

Andy got closer, and one of the guys caught his eye.

'Come on mate,' the main man said. 'Join in.'

46

Andy twitched at the thought of joining in, his cock getting a little hard again at the prospect of being inside Julie again. But he wasn't sure if she'd want him to.

He walked round to face her, and saw her eyes were closed, but she was moaning, panting. She opened her eyes and looked up at him.

'Fuck me,' she said, making Andy automatically get fully hard. He quickly got his cock out and said, 'Where do you want me?'

'My mouth,' she moaned. 'Fuck my mouth.'

He lifted her head, watching her full lips opening, then pushed the tip of his now very hard cock into her mouth. She began to suck it hungrily, her whole body jerking with the rhythm of the guys fucking her from behind. She sucked and licked it him as he took his cock out and ran it over her face. Then he pushed it in her mouth again and started fucking her mouth like it was her pussy. Her muffled moans of pleasure made his cock twitch and his orgasm build. He wanted to cum inside her so desperately.

As he rubbed his cock over her lips again, Julie said, 'Cum inside me. I want all your cum inside me.'

Andy couldn't hold anymore as her words had made his orgasm tingle all over him and right down to his twitching cock. He grabbed her hair and pushed his cock deep into her mouth and starting to push it in and out, moaning with the pleasure of fucking her. He looked at the other guys and heard them give grunts as they let go. That was it. Andy shot his cum into her mouth as she sucked and swallowed it. The other two guys filled her up with their cum as Julie cried out as her orgasm gripped her.

They all panted, while Julie lay there breathing hard, cum dripping from every part of her. She was used, satisfied. The two guys pulled out and started to get dressed.

'We've got to go,' one of them said as they all got ready to go. 'But we hope to see you here again one day.'

Andy helped Julie off the bonnet of their car, and back to hers. She got some clothes on, blushing as the others drove off, waving and beeping their horn.

When they were sat in silence in the car, Julie turned to Andy and said, 'Did that just really happen? Did I just get fucked by three men at the same time?'

'Yes, I think it did,' Andy said. 'How does it feel?'

'Would it be awful if I said I loved it?' she asked.

'Not at all. Would it be awful if I admitted I enjoyed it all too?'

She laughed. 'I bet you did.'

Then there was the sound of a loud Diesel engine coming towards them and tow truck appeared. It parked and the driver got out. To Andy he looked all right looking, quite broad, with tattooed arms.

'He's pretty hot,' Julie said. 'Wonder if he'd be up for some fun?'

Andy laughed, but he could see she was quite serious. 'Probably. I'm sure you could persuade him.'

Andy found himself in a lane in a wooded area, in a clearing. The rescue guy was in front of him, panting, his cock in Julie's mouth, fucking her hard. Andy had his hard cock in Julie's arse, his fingers inside her pussy. He was fucking her hard and she was loving it, moaning, groaning, wanting more.

Soon, Andy knew he was going to get to cum inside her again as his orgasm was building. It was the best lift of his life.

A NAUGHTY BEDTIME STORY

Clare settled under the covers, a cup of tea by her bed, feeling cosy. Next she took her phone off the side and opened up her Kindle app. She smiled, knowing what was awaiting her. There were now several stories, all of an erotic nature on her phone. They had been written and sent to her by her friend, Tony. Some of them were pretty hardcore, but she liked them anyway. She'd read them a few times, and decided to read them again. The stories were keeping her company while her other half, Rob was away working on the oil rigs. She had to get her pleasure somehow.

As she began, she slipped her free hand down her body, then into her knickers. She was wet already as she started to read, so pressed two fingers onto her clit, pressing a little, then swirling over it, feeling the pleasure rising over her, her nipples hardening as she began to read her favourite of his stories. She felt her juicy coating her fingers as she teased herself, her nipples growing hard as she read all the erotic moments of the book. She sank deep into the stories, enjoying the content. Then she fetched her vibrator, turned it on, still reading, letting it buzz as she teased between her legs, touching her clit, moaning a little.

Then her phone beeped.

She had a message. Who would be messaging her at this time? She checked what time it was and saw it was nearly ten pm. She'd just got comfy!

She looked at the text and saw it was from Tony. Tony! Why was he texting at this time?!

She read it. Tony: 'I'm outside xx'

Outside? What the bloody hell was he doing outside?

She got up, then put on her dressing gown, then went to the window and looked down on the street. There was someone standing there, so she peered closer. Yes, Tony was stood out the front of her house. The rain had started falling too, and he was huddled in a hooded coat.

She went downstairs, wondering all the time why he'd come to her house so late, feeling a bit of twinge in her back. It was a good job she was alone in the house tonight, she thought and opened the front door.

'Tony?' she said, looking up and down the street to make sure her neighbours weren't nosing about. 'What're you doing here?'

'Sorry,' he said coming closer to the door. 'I was just passing and thought I'd pop in.'

'But it's gone ten o'clock.'

'Is it?' he said and checked his phone. 'Oh yeah, sorry. Ok, I'll leave you to it.'

But the rain started hammering down as he started to go.

'Wait,' she said. 'You can't go home in this rain. You'll get soaked. Wait until it dries up. Come on.'

He smiled, then came up the steps. 'You sure?'

'Come in, you idiot. I'll make you a cup of tea.'

He went in and took his coat off while she headed into the kitchen to put the kettle on.

'I should put some clothes on really,' she said as she filled the kettle.

'Don't worry about that,' he said from the front room. 'I'll go when the rains stopped.'

She made the tea, then brought it into until lounge and found him sitting on the sofa.

'Thanks,' he said.

She smiled, then went over to the other sofa to sit down. She let out a pained cry when she went to sit down, an ache rippling down her back.

'You OK?' he asked, sitting up.

'Just my back, I think,' she said, rubbing her neck. 'Just aching a bit at the moment. I'll be fine.'

'You need a massage,' he said, sipping his tea.

'Oh yeah,' she said, laughing. 'Sounds lovely. But who's going to give me a massage?'

'I can do it,' he said, smiling.

She almost spat out her tea. 'You? You'll give me a massage?'

'Yeah, I'm very good at massages. I'll get your back feeling better.'

'I bet,' she said, looking at him suspiciously. 'Don't know if I can trust those hands of yours.'

'Oh come on,' he said, showing his empty palms. 'It's just a massage. I'll massage your back and you'll feel much better. I promise. You got any oil?'

'Yeah, but I'm not sure I should be letting you give me a massage.'

'Go on, get the oil. It'll be fine. Promise. You might need something to lie on too.'

She got up, still feeling unsure. But then her back was feeling pretty achey. And she could always tell him to stop if he did try anything on. 'All right, just a quick back massage. But that's it. I've got a little camp bed thing I can lay on.'

She went off to her bedroom, still feeling unsure, and fetched her camp bed and some towels and the massage oil.

When she came back, Tony helped her set up the bed, ready for her massage.

'Right, you better strip down,' he said.

'Hmm...I'll just take off my top, and leave my bra on.'

She took off her robe, leaving her pyjama bottoms on, then laid down on the table face down. She looked over at him as she saw him pick up the bottle of massage oil. 'Just behave yourself,' she said, then tried to relax.

'Just got to warm up the oil,' he said and she could hear the oil in his hands, the slipping, sliding noise of it.

Then she felt his hands on her, which felt strange, and laughed a little, giggling.

'What?' he said.

'Sorry,' she said. 'Just laughing. Can't believe you're giving me a massage.'

'Just relax,' he said, then pressed his hands along her back and spine, the oil coating her. It didn't feel too bad, kind of nice as he stared massaging, pressing her muscles with his hands, unknotting her back. It did feel like a relief to have someone helping her back, lifting the pain a little. She felt more oil being put over her back, then his hands expertly working it in, going from her back to her shoulders, and massaging her neck. It felt good and she could feel the tension leaving her body. It felt really good. 'That's nice,' she said.

'Good,' he said, working her back, rubbing the oil all over her neck, shoulders, down her spine. She felt his hands going lower, right down to the small of her back.

52

'I forgot you had this tattoo there,' he said.

She laughed as she felt his hands going further down, pulling a little at her pyjama bottoms, almost pulling them down.

'What you doing?' she said, turning her head to see him.

'Sorry, just need to lower your pyjama bottoms, so I can do your back properly.

'Hmm,' she said, but lowered her pyjama bottoms a little. The top of her bum and her thong would be showing, but that was all.

Then she felt more oil being dripped at the base of her spine, leaking down to her bum, being rub between the top of her arse cheeks. Then his hands were working her back, her lower back, going down, just stopping at the top of her bum. He smoothed the oil up her back and down, making her tingle all over and she could feel herself relaxing even more. It felt good, and didn't feel weird like she thought it might.

His hands expertly worked their way down, rubbing, massaging, oiling her skin, making the hairs stand up along her neck. His hands went down, down, massaging...then she felt his hands slide over her bum, massaging, rubbing...mmm it felt good. Then she realised his hands were on her bum!

'Hey, you, what do you think you're up to?' she said, resting on her elbows.

'It's ok. Just need to massage all the way down. It's no good doing just your back. Better lower your pyjama bottoms or take them off. Don't want to get oil on them.'

'Hmm,' she said. But it did seem to be working. Her back was starting to feel better. 'All right. But no funny business. Behave yourself! I don't think Rob would approve.'

He smiled, so she quickly got up, removed her pyjama bottoms and laid down again.

'You might want to unclip your bra,' he said. 'Don't want to get oil on that too.'

'All right,' she said, so undid it, and slipped it off. She laid down, resting her breasts on the towel covered bed.

Now she was only in her thong.

Tony started to pour oil all over her bum and legs. Then she felt his hands slowly working their way down sliding and rubbing the oil along her back, then sliding easily over her bum. She tingled a little at his touch as she felt his fingers dig deep in to her flesh, pushing, caressing her oiled bum. It felt good, better than it should. But she told herself it was ok. She would tell him off if he went too far.

His hands slipped down her legs, spreading the oil all over her muscles, her skin, working her flesh, making her body feel great, and relaxed. He slid his hands up the backs of her legs, then up to her bum, and down.

Then she felt his hands slip towards her thighs, massaging the inside of her legs, working up and down, working the oil over

her legs. His fingers and palms smoothed her oiled skin, making her warm, tingly all over as they reach up her inner thighs. His fingers stopped, just before they reached anything delicate. Then she felt his hands holding her legs and pushing them further apart.

'Now what're you doing?' she asked, still lying down.

'Just trying to massage your legs better,' he said. 'No funny business.'

'Behave,' she said, almost in a whisper as she felt oil being trickled on her inner thigh, then his warm hands on her again, twisting her thigh, the muscle, working up her legs again, making a warm sensation start and carry on up her body. His fingers worked up her inner thigh, but would stop short, not reaching between her legs. But she was aware of how close he was getting to THERE...

'Maybe that's enough now,' she said, hardly able to move, feeling very relaxed, her body still tingling.

'I need you to turn over though,' he said, so I can do your shoulders properly.'

'Turn over?! No way!'

'You can cover yourself up,' he said. 'I'll just quickly do your shoulders and that'll be that. Promise.'

'Hmm...' she said, eyeing him suspiciously. 'It better be. Right, turn away for a moment.'

He did as ordered, then she turned herself over and laid on her back. She put her hands over her breasts, covering her nipples. It would be ok, she told herself. He wouldn't dare misbehave himself.

She felt a dribble of oil being poured over her shoulders, then his hands touching them, kneading them, massaging. Then her neck, his finger tips palm squeezing, ironing out the knots. It did feel good. She heard herself letting out a little moan. She blushed a little as she felt his hands slide over her shoulders then over her breast bone, but stopping short of her hands that covered her breasts. His hands slid the oil all over her chest, apart from her breasts, kneading her arms, her shoulders, getting closer to her breasts all the time. Her arms started to relax, and she was hardly able to keep her breasts covered. She relaxed her hands a little, letting out a sigh, feeling his hands slip under her hands, massaging just round her breasts, coating her in the warm oil. It felt good, she felt nice all over, finding a soft moan coming from her mouth, while his hands slid round her breasts and shoulders, smoothing her skin.

Then his oiled hands were sliding over her breasts, coating them in oil, her arms having fallen to her sides. She was hardly aware she was now lying topless, her breasts exposed. When his oiled palms slid over and caressed her bare nipples, it made her tingle, and warm between her legs. It was just him being thorough, she told herself even though he poured more oil over her breasts and nipples, then began rubbing and squeezing them gently, oiling her nipples, massaging her bare breasts, making her whole body warm and sizzling.

She groaned a little with the pleasure, realising she should probably stop him. 'What you doing?' she managed to whisper.

'It's OK,' he said quietly, his hands still sliding, smoothing the oil over her breasts, his finger tips now teasing her nipples that had hardened. It was ok. It was ok, just a massage, she told herself even though a warmth had started to glow between her legs and travel and tingle all over her. One of his hands stayed over her left breast, oiling it, his palm smoothing over her nipple, while she felt his other hand oil her stomach, her abdomen. She felt his finger tips caress her belly button, sliding, oiling her body, her nipples hard. She let out a moan, feeling his other hand go lower, towards the centre of her legs, brushing the tiny triangle of hair she had there. More oil trickled over her body, down to her abdomen. Then his hand, rubbing, working her stomach right down, down, getting closer to between her legs. She tightened her thighs together as she felt his hands go deep, over the wisp of hair, just millimetres from her opening. 'Naughty,' she managed to say, but she could hardly move as the warmth, the tingling went from her nipples and all the way down.

'You'd better stop...' she said, in a half moan as his hand went up, then down, lower, lower, sliding over her stomach.

She felt his fingers gently brush over her opening, and she let out a sigh. Just a massage, she thought to herself. Only a massage. It was ok. Rob wouldn't object to her having a massage.

But she knew it wasn't ok when his fingers slid down, then over her opening, pushing apart the oily lips of her pussy. But she realised it wasn't just the oil coating her her pussy lips, but her juices. His hand slid up and down her oily wet lips, as a sigh, a groan slipped from her mouth. His fingers parted her wet lips, sliding over her hole, then up to her clit. He oiled her clit, his other hand still massaging her nipples.

She found her legs parting a little to allow his hand to slip between her legs and over the lips of her pussy. The pleasure rose over her, and she shut her eyes, kept them closed, telling herself it was ok, just a massage. But the tingle, the burning warmth and excitement raced up and over her, invading every part as his finger tips found her oily clit, teasing it, flicking it gently, swirling over it, sending pulse after pulse of pleasure to every inch of her body.

Then he seemed to stop for a moment, his hands withdrawing, and she found her pussy wanting, aching to have his hands back there even though she knew it was wrong. What was he doing?

His slipped her thong off, then his warm hands were back, sliding the oil all over her stomach and sliding between her legs, delving over her warm, wet slit, her pussy lips welcoming his touch while her nipples hardened and her mouth opened to let out a moan of pleasure.

She wondered why he'd momentarily stopped and she dared to open her eyes. Then she looked up to see that he'd removed his shirt. He was now bare chested. He'd obviously been working out, his chest seemed nice and chiselled, his arms quite muscular, his chest hair shaved off. She looked up at him, looking at his chest, letting out soft moans as his fingers worked her clit, then delved into her opening, dipping into her pussy.

She let out a deeper moan as his fingers slipped inside her, finding her mound, her g-spot, while his thumb swirled over her oily clit, sending spasms of pleasure and electricity through her. He then grabbed the bottle of oil, took her right hand and squeezed oil into it. Then he guided her hand to his chest and she knew what he wanted. While his other hand slid up and over her clit and into her pussy, he directed her oily hand over his front, making her finger tips massage his chest. She let him, seeming powerless to stop as the pleasure rose through her, an orgasm on its way. He moved her finger tips to his nipples. She knew what he wanted, so she began moving her own hand, then lifted her left hand too, turning her body over. He kept fingering her pussy, teasing her clit as she slid her oily hands over his chest, finding his hard nipples and teasing them. He let out a moan as she softly flicked them, stroked them. Then she looked down towards his crotch, and saw that his cock was rock hard in his jeans, straining to get out. She encircled his nipples, teased them, squeezed them a little, getting wetter as she heard him moan and felt his warm hand fingering her pussy.

Then he used one hand to start unbuttoning his flies, unzipping himself and then taking down his boxers shorts, allowing his now very hard and quite thick cock to spring out. Her eyes opened wider as she saw it was already shiny and wet and sticky with precum. She kept teasing his nipples, her eyes on his twitching, throbbing cock, feeling her pussy gush more oily juices knowing she'd made him so hard.

He got the bottle of oil and dripped some oil onto his hard cock. Then he took one of her hands and wrapped it round his warm cock, sliding the oil all over it, coating the shaft and head. He moved her hand, making her pull his cock, wanking him. She let him, feeling powerless to stop as his fingers were inside her, making an orgasm rise in her. So she carried on after he let go of her hand, grasping his cock gently, stroking it, oiling it up, smoothing her hand over the shaft, feeling it twitch at her touch. He moaned as she teased his nipples with one hand and stroked his cock with the other. More precum oozed from the end, and she used her thumb to wipe and rub it over the head, making him let out a deep moan.

Her orgasm was coming closer, spikes of pleasure firing through her, pulsing from her pussy, making her pant and moan. 'Oh...fuck...' she moaned, looking up at him, then down at his shiny oily cock. 'Oh...yes, fuck...I want to cum...'

He started finger fucking her harder, teasing her clit, making her buck. His cock twitched inches from her mouth. She moved closer, getting her lips close to the head of his cock, so close she could smell it, the delicious manly scent of it mixed with the oil. She opened her mouth, poked out her tongue, licking the tip, tasting his precum. Then she took the tip into her mouth, and began sucking, licking while her hand still teased his oily nipples. He moaned, beginning to thrust his cock into her mouth, while his hand teased her clit faster. Her orgasm was ready to burst, making her buck, and moan.

'Oh, shit...' he said, looking down at her as she hungrily sucked him. 'That's it...oh shit...oh Clare... suck me...oh god...'

She moaned too, gripping his shaft, lifting her head so she could look up at him while licking and sucking his cock up and down. She felt him finger fucking her deeper, harder.

'Oh, Tony...that's it, make me cum...please, make me cum,' she moaned, looking up at him. She was now so turned on.

'I will...oh, Clare, I'll make you cum...' he panted, delving more fingers inside her.

'Cum for me,' she said, feeling completely out of control. 'Cum in my mouth...'

Her orgasm arrived, bursting through her, making her shout as she thrust and wanked his cock, sucking it. He let out a sudden desperate groan, his cock twitching like mad. Then a burst of cum started shootng out, spraying towards her, hitting her lips, her face, and her tongue. She licked her lips then licked the rest of the cum from his cock while she lay there panting, her orgasm still drifting over her.

'You're so fucking naughty!' she said, blushing, but feeling satisfied.

'I know,' he said, smiling.

He'd just cum and it felt like the best cum ever. He'd managed to cum in her mouth while watching her naked body, and making her cum. His cock still twitched. But he wasn't done yet. He looked over her oily, glistening body, then between her legs, parting them, and looking at her opening, the glistening wet lips of her delicious pussy.

'Now what do you think you're doing?' she said, trying to close her legs.

But he pushed them open again, getting his mouth close to her pussy, looking at her shiny clit, smelling her pussy. He licked, right up her opening, then sucked gently on her clit. He tasted her, the honeyed flavour of her, smelling the scent of the oil mixing with her juices. He delved his tongue inside her, then up to her clit, encircling it, teasing it, his cock hardening as he heard her let out a moan of pleasure. He put his hand over her pussy as he kept licking her clit, then pressed his fingers deep inside her, feeling she was now soaking wet. He pushed two fingers inside, finding her g-spot, making her groan and cry out, and buck as his tongue also teased her clit.

'Oh...yes...oh fuck...that's it...' she moaned, making his cock swell and get very hard again.

'Turn over,' he said, and she did, sliding on to her front. He got a couple of cushions and put them under her, lifting her bum in the air, allowing him a perfect view of her glistening oily pussy and, when he pulled her arse cheeks apart, her tight little hole. He slipped his hand to her pussy, teasing her clit, making her moan and buck, then grabbed the bottle of oil and poured some over her tight little puckered hole. It glistened as he teased her clit and fingered fucked her with two, three and then four fingers.

'Yes...fuck me...yes, Tony...oh fuck,' she groaned, pushed her pussy down towards his hand, grinding against his fingers.

With his other hand he slid his oily fingers down the crack of her arse and over her tight little hole, making her sigh and twitch. He teased her hole, then pushed two fingers gently in. 'Oh...you're naughty,' she panted as he pushed another finger in her tight hole while finger fucking her pussy.

'You like that, Clare?' he asked, fingering her tight hole, then licking her clit.

'Oh...fuck...keep fingering me...' she groaned, pushing her arse and pussy closer to him. He did, and tongued her pussy, then took out his fingers from her arse and got his mouth between her arse cheeks. He licked her puckered hole, then delved his tongue in there, making her squirm and pant and moan.

'My god...yes...please...make me cum!' she moaned.

His cock was so hard now and he couldn't hold back any longer. He got up on the bed, getting between her legs, pulling her arse towards him. His oily cock glistened as he pushed it towards her pussy. His cock sank in with a soft moan from her as she pushed back, making his cock sink deeper. He used his hand to massage her oily tight hole and pressed his fingers into it. She moaned louder, telling him to fuck her more and harder. He rammed his cock deep into her, out and in, hard and fast, hearing her beg for it, beg for her orgasm. Then he slid his cock out and slid it over her arse and pressed it into her tight hole. She cried out as he thrust it in, finding it slippery and oily.

'Oh fuck!' Clare panted as he started fucking her arse, ramming it in hard, wanting to shoot his cum into her.

Then she said, 'You lay down!'

She moved, letting him lie back as she climbed over his crotch, and grabbing his oily cock and pulling it towards her opening. She slid down over his rock hard cock, gripping it with her muscles. He let out a groan as he watched her oily, glistening body jerk and ride his cock. Her breasts and nipples shone as she pushed herself down on his cock, riding him faster and faster.

He found her clit and started teasing it, making her moan, and cry out as she rode him faster.

Then she leaned back, and put out her hands, and found his chest, then his oily nipples. She started stroking them as she ground her pussy over him, making his cock twitch and ache to cum. His nipples sent a wave of pleasure to his cock as he looked up into her face and saw her looking down at him, the pleasure stamped into her face.

'Tony...I'm going to...I'm going to cum! Fuck me!' she practically screamed.

'I'm going to cum too,' he panted, feeling his cock about to shoot his cum deep inside her.

'Oh fuck...oh god, I'm cuming!' she shouted, and he came to, feeling a big spurt of cum shoot deep inside her.

They panted, exhausted. Tony looked up at her, saw she was red faced.

'I can't believe you just seduced me,' she said. 'You're very bad man.'

'I know,' he said. 'It'll be our little secret.'

HER DIRTY BIRTHDAY SURPRISE

Maria pulled up, after finding the right address in the street. She saw his white door, the right number, then pulled on the handbrake. She adjusted her long dark hair in the mirror, straightened her short skirt, black leggings, and her red jumper. She wore her fur lined boots too. The get together for her birthday wasn't until later, so she had plenty of time to do this favour for her friend, Rich. She left the car and headed up the steps to his house, then rang the bell.

Rich opened the door smiling. 'You didn't really have to come round, not on your birthday, Maria.'

'What are friends for?' she said as she went into his house. 'And anyway, you promised me a birthday surprise!'

'Oh yeah, I did,' Rich said, as they headed into his large lounge. 'I hadn't forgotten.'

'I was only joking,' she said as she sat down on the leather sofa. 'I don't expect anything. Where's this picture you wanted help hanging?'

'Over there.'

Rich went over to the dining room where there was a large framed picture and some tools on the floor.

She followed. 'Where's your wife? At work?'

'She's gone away for a few days to visit her family in London.'

'OK. If I get a chair, I can hold the picture up and you can tell me where it needs to go.'

Rich fetched her a chair, so she got up on it, facing the wall. He handed her the framed picture, so she held it up against the wall.

'How's this?' Maria asked, but Rich was staring up at her, his eyes travelling up her long legs, then into the darkness beneath her short skirt, imagining what lay beneath there.

He'd planned the whole thing, decided to get her round to help him for this very reason. He moved closer, getting within arms reach.

'What do you think?' she asked. 'Rich?'

He reached out and put his hand on her bum, then the other hand, and squeezed a little. She flinched, turning round, looking shocked down at him but still holding the picture.

'What was that?!' she said. 'Did you just grab my bum?'

'I was just steadying you,' he said, lying. 'I thought you were going to fall.'

She looked at him suspiciously. 'Yeah, right, I know you mister! Cheeky. If you weren't my friend...'

He smiled, then got on with fixing the picture to the wall.

When they were done, he told Maria to sit in the living room, while he'd fetch her a cup of tea. But he didn't only make her a cup of tea, he brought in the birthday cake he had bought.

'Here you go,' Rich said, bring it in on a dish.

She sat up surprised. 'You got me a cake? You

didn't have to do that, you wally!'

'It's no problem. I also got you a couple of presents.'

'You didn't?'

'I did. Here.' Rich handed her the first wrapped present, which she took and examined.

She shook her head. 'You shouldn't have got me anything! You're silly.'

'Open it!'

She tutted, then began ripping the paper off, revealing a red, thin box inside. Then she opened it, and her eyes opened wide. 'Is this...have you got me...?'

'Do you like them?'

Maria lifted out a mesh, almost see through, basque and some stockings. 'I can't believe you bought this for me! What am I supposed to do with this?!'

'Put it on.' He smiled, watching her as she looked up at him, shocked.

'I'm not putting this on! You're married!'

'Go on. Just for me.'

'No, I can't. It wouldn't be right.'

'Go on, I was thinking of getting one for my wife, and she's about the same size as you. You can have that one.'

She stared at him, then the outfit. 'I'd look stupid...'

'You'll look great. Trust me. You'll be helping me out, trying it on.'

She looked at him through her narrowed, suspicious brown eyes. 'I'll put it on for two minutes, then that's it. You see if it fits ok and then I take it off. Promise?'

'I promise.'

Then Maria huffed, then disappeared out of the room and up the stairs. He waited, growing excited, unable to contain himself.

He couldn't wait to see her in it.

Then he heard her coming down the stairs, then into the front room. But he was disappointed to see she was wearing his robe over the outfit.

'I borrowed your dressing gown,' she said, blushing.

'Let's see. Please.'

She looked at him through narrowed hateful eyes as she slowly lowered the robe, revealing her body adorned in the black lacy and mesh basque, that barely hid her breasts. He could see her nipples, which looked quite hard. She was wearing the matching thong and the black sheer stockings. His cock twitched in his trousers, getting very hard.

'Turn round,' he said.

'No!'

'Please.' He smiled.

She huffed, but slowly turned round, making Rich gasp as he saw her bare, shapely bum, and the thong she was barely wearing.

'You look so fucking sexy,' he groaned.

'Yeah, right. Now I'm taking it all off.'

But when she turned round, he had his mobile out and took a couple of snaps of her.

'What you doing?!' she shouted. 'You better delete that!'

'I will. I promise, later.' He smiled.

'What does that mean? What're you up to?'

'I just want you to do a couple of things for me first...'

'Like what?'

'I want you to eat some cake.' He cut Maria a large piece.

'You want me to eat cake?'

He nodded, then undid his trousers, showing off his now very swollen, hard, and glistening cock. He inserted his cock into the cake and rested it on his lap. 'Now you eat it.'

'You are joking?!' She looked pissed off, shocked, but still very horny in the sexy outfit.

'No, I'm not. Do this and I'll delete the photo.'

She narrowed her eyes. 'You'd better!'

Then he smiled, his cock twitching with excitement as she knelt next him on the sofa, getting on all fours, lowering her head towards the cake.

'You're a bastard,' she said, shaking her head.

'Eat some cake.'

She lowered her head, opening her luscious full lips, her tongue poking out to scoop up some cream. His cock throbbed, waiting, seeing her eat cake and lick up the cream. Then his eyes fell to her bum that was raised in the air. He slowly placed as hand on her bum, gently squeezing.

'Behave, you,' she said, but her next lick hit the tip of his cock, and he sighed with pleasure, making him grip her bum firmer.

He pushed himself up, pressing his hard cock closer to her face.

'Lick the cream off,' he panted.

'No!'

He gave her bum a spank and he thought he heard a moan from her lips, so he did it again, a little harder and squeezed. Her mouth went down, her tongue darting out and lapping the cream and cake from his cock. He shuddered, feeling the pleasure of it and staring at her bum and her long legs in the stockings she was wearing. Her mouth opened again, then slipped round the head of his cock and started to suck gently. The pleasure raced through him.

'Oh, fuck...yes, Maria...' he moaned as she kissed and licked the tip and the underside. Then her full lips kissed it up and down, taking the cake away, making his cock tremble and throb. He slapped her arse a couple of times and heard her give a gasp. Then he ran his hand to her leg, along her thigh to the thong, and cupped her. She bucked a little, pulling away, but he pressed his hand there and felt she was quite wet. He started using his fingers to tease her, rubbing them along the wet slit of her pussy, then toying with her clit.

She moaned a little, then said, 'Behave you!'

But he didn't, just pushed his finger firmer to her clit, stroking it, swirling round it, making her buck and moan as she started to suck his cock with hunger. Then he used his other hand to move the thong from her arse, then slowly run his fingers along the crack. She jerked a little but he worked her clit and made her moan louder.

'Sit astride me,' he said, so she moved, turning and putting her knees either side of him, her pussy nearly over his hard, throbbing cock. Now he could see her breasts through the mesh material, making him ache. He unbuttoned his shirt, revealing his chest. 'Touch my chest.'

'You should be behaving yourself,' she said, but her long fingers touched his chest, caressed him all over, her big brown eyes half closed, watching him, knowing what he wanted.

Slowly her fingers encircled his hard nipples, making him let out a moan.

Then she caressed them, stroking his nipples, making his cock stiffen and precum ooze from the tip.

'Oh yes, Maria,' he gasped. 'Fuck...I want you.'

Then he slipped his hand under her, cupping her pussy, and pulling aside her thong. Her soaking wet opening fell on his hand, so he pushed two fingers inside her, while his other hand found her tight little hole. She groaned when he teased her anus and delved a finger in and out, using her juices from her pussy to lubricate her.

'This...is...' she managed to pant. 'Wrong...we shouldn't be doing this.'

But he put a third finger into her now oily wet pussy, finding her g-spot and teasing it.

'Stop...' she groaned. 'You're married, Oh fuck...'

Rich kept finger fucking her, feeling her juicies flowing and coating his hands, making her pant and squirm. He reached his head forward, opening his mouth, finding her right hard nipple and licked it, sucked it gently. She moaned more.

'Say you want my cock inside you...' Rich groaned.

'I can't...it's wrong...we have to stop...'

He caressed her g-spot, finding her clit his thumb. She gasped, 'Oh shit, no, oh god...fuck...'

'Say it, say you want my cock inside you...'

'No, I can't...'

He put four fingers in her, still working her clit and put two fingers of his other hand into her tight little hole.

She let out a massive moan, then groaned. 'You bastard, oh fuck...I want your cock inside me...'

He smiled. 'Not yet, Maria. I'll make you beg for it.'

He slapped her arse, making her moan. 'Now I want your beautiful lips round my cock again.'

She moved to the floor, getting between his legs, then hungrily taking his cock into her mouth, looking up at him with her big brown eyes as she tongued the tip, sucked it, licked it up and down, kissed his cock like it was his mouth. He felt his cock shudder as the realisation that she was doing everything he'd fantasised about. And she was loving it. She was so wet.

He wanted to cum, and she must have felt it, because she looked up and said, 'Cum in my mouth. I want your warm cum in my mouth.'

That was all he needed as she sucked again, making his orgasm build right through him until his cock ached, then twitched madly and let a jet of cum burst out of him. She leaned back a bit, opening her full lips. His cum sprayed over her mouth, over her lips and into her mouth. She licked her lips and smiled.

'Feel better?' she asked.

He nodded.

'You're still a bastard,' she said.

'Maybe. Want to get me back?'

She half closed her eyes again. 'How?'

He took out another present from next to the sofa. 'For you.'

'What? What now?' She quickly unwrapped it, revealing a large rectangular box.

'Open it,' he said, smiling.

She did and her eyes widened. 'Really?'

She pulled the large pink dildo from the box. At one end it was like a large pink cock, at the other end it curled in.

'It's a strapless strapon,' he said. 'That end goes in you...the other...'

She smiled. 'My revenge. Turn over,' she said.

He watched her attached it, sliding the end into her, so the big cock end pointed out straight out in front of her. He was feeling a little regret at this point. But it was too late to go back now.

'Go on, get on all fours,' she said.

He did, waiting. Then he felt wetness, the cold lube being smeared over his tight hole. It sent a shiver of pleasure over him, making his cock get a little hard again.

Then he felt it, the tip of the dildo press against his lubed arse, Maria slowly forcing her way in.

'Hows that?' she asked.

'Not too bad,' he said. It did feel pretty good. Then there was a surge of uncomfortable pain as she pushed the dildo right inside of him.

'Does that hurt?' she asked.

'Yes.'

'Good.' Then she pulled out and he felt pleasure fill him up. She thrust in and out, and he could feel her warm breath on his back as she started to pant, moaning a little as the bit inside her started to do its thing.

'You want me to fuck your tight hole, don't you?' she asked. 'Yes, Maria, fuck me.'

She did, she push deep in, slowly out, fucking him, her hands gripping his hips, pulling him back.

It felt so good. Painful, but his cock grew big and throbbed again as she pushed in and pulled out. Now her hands reached round him as he felt her breasts push against his back.

Her fingers found his nipples and she began to tease them as she thrust in and out of him. He felt the surge of another orgasm overtake him, listening to her moaning herself as the other end of the dildo fucked her.

'Oh fuck, Maria,' he moaned, 'I'm going to cum!'

'Wait!' she said. 'Turn round!'

She pulled out, then put her mouth to his cock as it twitched and began to spew more cum into her open mouth. She licked the rest of the cum off him, then looked up at him.

'Now you've got to make me cum,' she said, looking at him with narrowed eyes.

'I've got another birthday surprise for you,' he said, smiling, then text something on his phone.

A little while later he went to the door. He came back into the room followed by two men. They were quite muscular, tattoos around their thick arms. They both sort of resembled Ray Liotta, she decided. There was something quite horny about them both.

'What's going on?' she asked, feeling a little nervous, and covering herself up with her hands.'

'These two are your birthday treat,' Rich said, sitting down. 'Enjoy.'

'What?' she said as the two men started taking off their tops, showing off their lean muscular bodies. One of them grabbed her arse, the other her face and started kissing her.

His tongue entered her mouth as she tried to protest. Then the other man's large hand was between her legs, clamping on her still wet pussy. His fingers found her clit and started working it as the other guy kissed her, his hands finding her nipples and teasing them. She found herself kissing the guy back, and moaning into his mouth as the the other guy finger fucked her. When she looked over at Rich, she could see he was watching, stroking his cock, making it hard again.

Then she was lifted onto the other sofa, laid down, with one of the men at either end. The next thing she knew, the man in front of her had his thick, hard and tanned cock out and was pushing it towards her mouth. Behind her, the other guy fingered her pussy and arse, making her moan. The cock slipped between her lips, sliding in and out, fucking he mouth. Pleasure sank into her. Then she bucked when she felt another hard cock pushing against her tight hole. It went in, and she moaned, and started hungrily sucking the cock in her mouth. The man moaned, while the guy behind pushed in and out of her tight hole, making an electric stream of pleasure tear through her. Her orgasm began, tingling all over her, making her pussy gush with juices.

'I'm cuming!' she cried and moaned as she came, crying out. The two guys jerked and throbbed too, and she suddenly felt both their cocks spurt cum, filling her up. She collapsed to the sofa, feeling used but almost satisfied as the guys got up.

At sometime they must have left, because it was just her and Rich again. He was stood by the sofa, hard as the first time. 'Now do you want my cock?' he asked.

'Yes, please,' she said.

He climbed on top of her, pushing his cock into her wetness, and she felt him shudder inside her as he filled her up. She put her legs round him as he thrust deep into her, making her moan. He kissed her, and she kissed him back, her tongue teasing his.

His fingers teased her clit as he thrust in and out of her, another orgasm building.

'Fuck me, Rich...please fuck me,' Maria said...

'Don't want me to behave?'

'Not right now. Just fuck me...'

'Happy birthday,' he said, pushing deep inside her.

THE NIGHT OUT

Sarah dabbed some perfume behind her ears and turned to look at herself in the long mirror. She looked good in her black dress and black tights. She slipped on her boots and finished doing her make-up. She picked up her phone and saw she had a message from Jess: 'Meeting at the Fort at 8. See u then x.' She smiled and saw she had a message on Twitter. She knew who it was from already and decided to look anyway. Yep, it was from Paul, the older guy who sat opposite her at work. They'd struck up a kind of friendship lately, which was nice, but lately he'd become a bit of a nuisance. It was the way he stared at her sometimes, and there were moments when she had caught him watching her as she walked away from their desk. Yes, there was part of her that was attracted to him, but she was married and found herself promising herself to stay away from him. The problem now was that Jess had arranged a night out for them all, a bit of a pub crawl ending up in a club. Paul was coming along. She would have to stay away from him all night.

Paul's message said: 'Looking forward to tonight. Should be fun ;-) xx.'

She tutted and rolled her eyes. She knew what was

on his mind, but he was sorely mistaken. She shrugged off the matter and decided to concentrate on having a great night.

The house was empty for once, so she relaxed, had a nice chilled glass of white while she waited for the taxi to come. She thought about who would be coming tonight- Amy, Jess, Tim and Ian. How Ian got permission to come out, she didn't know, but she was glad in a way. Then her mind turned back to Paul, and she felt a little annoyed at Jess for inviting him- obviously she didn't understand the full extent of Paul's obsession, although she did understand that the two of them had flirted in the past.

With her third glass of wine down her neck, the cab tooted outside and she quickly locked up and ran out and jumped into minicab.

The Fortesque was quite packed and she had to squeeze through the students and professional boozers so she could try and spot her crowd. She smiled when she saw Ian, done up in smart black jeans and a salmon polo shirt. She could smell his aftershave when she was still a few feet away. Amy wore a little dark red dress and thick wool coat.

'Alright, Sarah,' Ian said, raising his pint of ale.

'I'm alright, Ian,' she said, looking at them both. 'What've you two been gossiping about?'

Ian smirked, but Amy just grinned and said, 'We were wondering if any of us would do anything silly tonight.'

'Silly?' Sarah said. 'What does that mean?'

Ian winked at her. 'You know. Will any of us put our fingers in any pies.'

Amy spat out her drink as she sipped it and

doubled over laughing.

'No one's fingering my pie,' Sarah said, laughing too. 'Ian, you have a wonderful way with words.'

'I know. I'm like the new Shakespeare, innit?'

'You are, you are,' Sarah said. 'Where's Tim?'

'That's not who I thought you'd ask about,' Amy said, smirking. 'I thought you'd be wondering where Paul is.'

'Tell me he isn't coming,' she said.

'I'm afraid he is,' Amy said.

'What's happened?' Ian asked.

Amy looked at him. 'How do you not know that Paul has a thing for Sarah? He keeps staring at her and saying dodgy things.' 'Does he?' Ian said.

'Yeah, he does,' Sarah said. 'The bastard stares at me across the pod.'

Ian laughed. 'Undressing you with his eyes. He does it to me all the time.'

'Does he? I'd like to see him undress you for real!' Sarah laughed.

'Cheeky cow,' Ian said.

'Hi,' Jess said and joined the crowd. She already had a pint of real ale in her hand. 'I thought I'd be the first one here.'

'Here comes Mr Marston,' Ian said pointing over their heads. 'Alright, Mr Watt?' Paul said and pushed through the crowd. 'Hey, Sarah,you alright?'

Sarah looked away, but said, 'Yeah, I'm good, thanks.'

'Right, shall we find somewhere to sit seeing as we're all here?' Amy said, smiling brightly.

'There's that table over there, opposite the bar.' Ian pointed across the bar, then headed over and they all followed. Paul and Ian were the first ones to reach the table and slid under it, facing the bar. Sarah regretted taking her time to go over, stoping to get another drink. When she reached the table she saw that the girls had taken up the rest of the seats. There was nowhere for her to sit.

'Where I am I suppose to sit?' she said.

'You can squeeze in,' Ian said.

'You can sit on my lap,' Paul said and smiled.

'Thanks, but I don't think so.' She suddenly found herself having to move closer to Paul when a crowd of young drinkers swarmed past.

She suddenly found Paul's arm round her waste and pulling her on to his lap. She lost balance and found herself letting him pull her onto his knees.

'There you go, Sarah,' Jess said, and winked.

'Thanks, but I'm not sitting on your lap, Paul.' Sarah tried to get off his lap, but found one of Paul's arms tightly wrapped around her waist. 'Let me up.'

'No,' Paul whispered in her ear.

She looked around the at the rest of the gang for support, but everyone was chatting and joking among themselves.

Then she jerked a little as she felt Paul's hands grasp her backside. He grabbed her tightly, digging his fingers into her cheeks.

'Stop it,' she said, but not too loudly as she didn't want to make a scene.

'No way,' he said, and squeezed again. 'I've got you where I want you. And if you try and move, maybe I'll spread rumours around work about us.'

'You wouldn't dare.'

'Wouldn't I?'

She looked round at him and saw that he had one eyebrow raised. He was an evil sod, she thought. She decided to remain where she was as she couldn't risk rumours at work.

'Where we going after this?' Ian asked, then started texting on his phone.

'The Junction,' Jess said. 'There's a band on I want to see.'

'What band?' Sarah asked, then felt something under her. Her heart raced and she felt herself blushing as she realised that Paul's hand had found its way under her and then between her legs. It was resting there, but she could feel it just by her thigh. 'What're you doing?' she whispered.

'Nothing,' Paul said, a laugh in his voice.

'You better move your hand,' she whispered.

But he didn't, and then she felt his palm brush along the nylon covering her warm thigh. He stopped and went back towards her knee again and she breathed a sigh of relief. Then his hand was moving back again between her legs. His hand stopped, so close, now trembling a little. She was ready to jump up and make the excuse of going to the bar, but she had nearly a full glass of wine sitting in front of her.

She clamped her legs shut when she felt his hand slip closer, ready to cup her. He was struggling, pushing his hand further up her leg, so close to touching her... Then the fingers of his other hand grasped tightly at her arse again, and she jumped a little when she felt his teeth bite at her back. She tried to wriggle away from his hand, but she'd carelessly forgotten about his other hand. He took his chance and slid his hand between her legs and nestled in, his warm palm pressed against where her slit would be, hidden by her tights and knickers. She bit her lip and subtlety tried to lift herself away from his hand, but his fingers gently began to encircle her clit.

'Stop it!' she hissed.

'No. I won't. I want to make you come.'

'You can't. I don't want you to.'

But his fingers dug in more, finding her clit while his thumb pressed towards her silky opening. She could feel him pushing, as if a small cock was trying to gain entry. As his fingers began to press firmer on her clit, she could feel it going against her wishes and becoming erect. That was the human body, she told herself, it reacted like that. It wasn't her fault. That's what she kept saying as her nipples hardened and pressed against her bra. Then she felt the wetness spreading down through her knickers and her tights. She felt him smear his fingers with her wetness, then pull his hand away. When she looked around he licked his fingers and smiled at her.

He didn't try anything more in that pub. Somebody announced it was time to drink up and then they all headed outside and hurried up the road towards the junction pub. Half angry at herself at getting wet, and furious at Paul for touching her up, she slowed down and walked beside him. He'd obviously let himself fall back from the crowd, and she decided, with suspicion that he'd planned for her to approach him for a confrontation.

She punched his arm and said, 'I can't believe you did that!'

'You liked it,' he said, grinning. 'You got all wet. You tasted great.'

'Fuck off. You took advantage of me! Don't you dare do that again!'

'I might not do that again. But I'm not going to stop until you're on your knees, with your beautiful mouth around my cock.' She stood there, blank, shocked by his words as he laughed and hurried off towards the pub.

Inside the pub it was heaving. A horde of sweating bodies filled the place, most adorned in black with long hair. A heavy metal band were playing, the beat and guitars roaring out to her ears. She looked round the pub, trying to spot the gang. She couldn't see anyone at first, especially not Paul, who she was keeping a careful eye out for. She was feeling a little ashamed. She had got wet and now, when she thought of what he had done, she found herself becoming aroused. What was wrong with her?

She smiled with relief when she saw nearly the whole gang at the corner of the bar and pushed through the crowd to get to them.

'Where did you go?' Jess asked, paying the barman. 'Last time I saw you, you were talking to Paul.'

'Yeah, we were just chatting,' she said and blushed a little. 'Where is he?'

Jess picked up a glass of whisky and sipped it. 'Don't know. Didn't see him come in. Maybe he went home.'

'I hope so,' Sarah whispered to herself. All it needed was for someone from work seeing Paul feeling her up and the word would get out. She needed to be forceful with him, to make sure he got the message that nothing could go on. She was about to get served when the barman disappeared. She saw him head over the otherside and followed him and managed to find a gap in the two layers of people. Everyone hedged her in and she was trapped, her money in her hand. As she looked to see Jess, and find where the rest of the gang had got to, she felt that someone was behind her. They were quite close and probably wanted to get to the bar, but she had nowhere to go to. Then she felt them getting closer and almost felt their breath on her neck. Then they moved really close, now pressing themselves against her. They were pressing firmly against her, and she could feel their crotch digging into her backside.

'Oi,' she started to say and turned her head. Paul was wearing a smile as he put his arms round her waist, pushing his groin closer to her, rubbing himself against her arse. She could feel that he was getting aroused, his erection obviously growing as he rubbed himself against her backside.

She tried to move, but she was trapped. There were too many bodies surrounding her, and nobody would hear her if she called out to them. Paul suddenly bit into her neck, nibbling, then sucking, and then kissing up to her ear.

'Get off,' she said, her voice barely a whisper.

'Can you feel how hard I am?' he asked.

She could. He was as hard as anyone she'd ever felt pressed against her. She could almost feel the throb of him as he pushed against her. Then his hands lifted up her skirt and ran all over her arse, squeezing, grabbing, his finger tips biting into her cheeks. Then she felt it, the warmth of arousal. No, it was wrong.

'Stop it!' She growled.

But he slipped his hand between her legs, his finger tips stroking her gusset, pushing up into her slit. He pulled his hand back and used his thumb to stroke her anus. She bucked a little and he pressed harder against her tight hole. Her body did it again- betrayed her- by allowing her to become wet. She felt a shudder of pleasure as he pressed his thumb against her tight hole while his finger tips dipped towards her now wet pussy.

'I want to put my cock in your tight hole,' he whispered into her ear, then sucked and kissed her neck.

'Don't...please stop, Paul, please. Please stop.' But she let out a moan.

'No. I want you to beg me to fuck you. I want to hear you beg me to fuck you in every hole you've got.'

'I can't. Get off me!'

Then Ian pushed through the crowd and stood next to Sarah, seemingly unaware of what was being done to her, and how wet she had got.

'You Ok, Sarah?' Ian asked.

She felt Paul slip away from her and sink back into the crowd. But she could still feel his thumb as if it was still pressed between her arse cheeks, and his fingers still searching her wetness.

'I'm OK now, Ian, thanks,' she said, adjusting her skirt.

'Thanks for what?' he asked.

'Nothing. It's Ok.'

It was Amy's idea to go to a club, so they all jumped into a cab and headed into town. All the time, she tried not to make eye contact with Paul, but it was hard not to. She quickly looked his way and saw he had an evil glint in his eye.

They queued up outside the first club they came to and were soon ushered inside. They all rushed up the ramp that would take them to the centre of the club as the heavy and fast beat of music blasted at their ears. Strobe lights flickered over the glittering bodies that were crammed into the dance floor. Jess and Amy shouted something into her ears, but she couldn't hear what they said. They pointed to the bar and she nodded and followed them as they squeezed past the sweaty, dancing crowds. She could see Ian was dancing, throwing shapes here and there. Perhaps he'd popped a pill, she thought and laughed.

Again, Paul was nowhere to be seen, which put her on edge. When Jess made the international sign language for 'Do you want a drink?' Sarah nodded and pointed to the toilets.

She wanted to freshen herself up and get some peace from the thud of music.

When she got into the toilets, she found a few women queuing, but soon a cubicle came free and she went to slip inside. When she went to shut the door, she found the door wouldn't move. She looked round and saw Paul was holding it open.

'What the fuck do you think you're doing?' she shouted.

He took out his mobile phone and took a picture. 'Now I've got a nice photo of you in a cubicle. People will wonder how I managed that.'

'Fuck off!' She took a swipe at him, but Paul dodged out of the way. Then he turned and took a selfy of them both.

'You better delete that, you bastard.'

Paul smiled. 'Just emailed it to myself. Now if that was to find itself on Facebook...'

'You wouldn't dare...' Sarah said, and tried to snatch away his phone.

'Like I said, I've emailed it to myself. I can put it on Facebook anytime I like.'

'Don't even joke about it, Paul.'

He smiled and put away his phone. 'I'm not. I won't put it on Facebook, unless you do something for me.'

Her stomach turned over as he spoke and her heart began to beat a lot faster. Something bad was coming. 'What?'

'First, take off your tights, then your knickers and

then put your tights back on.'

She shook her head. 'No way. You're fucking mad if you think I'll do that.'

'OK, then I'll just post the pic of us on Facebook. All I'm asking you to do is take off your knickers.'

She had little choice. She couldn't risk him posting the photograph and anyone seeing it and telling on her. 'You better turn around.'

'That's a good girl.' Paul turned round and faced the door.

She quickly slipped off her boots, then sat down and rolled down her tights, then took off her black underwear and put them in her handbag. Then she quickly pulled on her tights again and sat down on the toilet lid. 'Now what? Can I go now?'

'No way. I need to check you did it.'

'Oh come on, Paul, I could get in trouble. Just leave me alone, please.'

'I want to hear you beg, but not to be left alone. Now, open your legs. I want to make sure you took your knickers off.'

She shook her head, shaking a little, then slowly opened her legs. If she could placate him a little, then he might go away. Did she want him to go away? Why had she got so wet before?

'Wider!' he commanded.

She did as she was told, and she looked up to see him staring between her legs.

'That's better. Now I can see your beautiful pussy. Is it wet?'

She shook her head. 'No.'

'I want you to be wet. Touch yourself. Touch your pussy, stroke it. Make it wet.'

'Paul, I can't... It's wrong.'

'You haven't got much choice.'

Sarah started to tremble, the guilt swallowing her up as she slipped her hand between her legs and found the lips of her pussy through her tights. She brushed her fingers down her slit, and pushed in a little and then back up to her clit.

'That's it, stroke yourself,' Paul said, breathlessly.

She didn't look at him, she couldn't, just began to finger herself, putting two fingers on her clit and swirling around it.

'I bet that feels good,' Paul said and started to unbutton his jeans. He opened his boxer shorts and pulled out his now swollen cock. She saw his hand wrap around it, squeezing, and making the head of it bulge, and a drip of pre-cum ooze from the tip. She could see his erection grow twice as hard as it throbbed towards her. He began to tug his cock, jerking it back and forth, making more precum drip from the tip. He stepped closer and now she could see how rock hard he was as he stared between her legs.

'Don't stop, Sarah,' he said, breathing hard. 'I want to cum looking at you.'

'Just hurry up,' she said, and fingered her clit, finding it stiffen under her touch. The nylon was stretched over it, making the touch of it even more smooth. She looked up again and saw him, open mouthed, stroking his cock, pumping it hard, then softly. She could see his erection twitching, his legs spasm as the pleasure pulsed through him. There was something about him, about him watching her and seeing his cock so engorged as he pleasured himself that gave her satisfaction. She felt warm and tingly to have the power- then the wetness soaked through from her open pussy and coated her tights. She played with herself, stroking herself in time with the movements of his hand as it stroked his cock up and down. He stepped closer again, his cock glistening with precum. She was suddenly concerned he might try and touch her with his erection- she couldn't have that- that would be terrible. So bad. Wrong.

So, she began to touch herself more, making herself more wet, just so he might come quicker.

'Stand up,' he said, still pulling hard on his cock.

'Why?'

'Just do it... Remember I have the photo!'

She stood up slowly, feeling strange, a little turned on despite the guilt and shame. It was the power she had over him, making him so hard and crazy with desire.

'Now turn round and bend over.'

'What? No!'

'Do it, Sarah.'

What choice did she have? It wasn't like she was actually touching him. She turned round and bent over, waiting, ready to hit him if he came near her. As much as she was now turned on, she still knew it was wrong.

'Drop your skirt.'

She did what he said, starting to shake. She looked over her shoulder and saw him stroking his hard cock, his mouth open and panting. He was jerking it madly. 'Part your cheeks. I want to see your tight hole through your tights.'

'Paul!'

'Do it.'

She swallowed, then put her hands on her cheeks and pulled them apart. She felt her hole touch the nylon, and heard the soft wet noise of Paul tugging himself even more.

'Finger your pussy,' he commanded.

She slipped her hand between her legs and began

to finger her pussy again, feeling it still so wet. She pushed her fingers against her gushing pussy and spread the wetness up to her clit. Her tights were soaked now and she could smell her juices and his warm cock. He was close behind, bulging, nearly ready to come, breathing hard, saying her name in a whisper: 'Sarah, Sarah, I want to slide into your pussy.'

She felt a little electricity pulse through her pussy at hearing his words. No, she thought, it's wrong, I can't let myself get turned on. But her slit was oozing with her juices, and her nipples were so stiff now.

She felt a sudden dab of wetness between her arse cheeks and turned to see Paul tonguing her arse.

She pulled away from him, shocked by what he had done. She was trembling as she pulled up her skirt and then pushed past him and ran out through the club.

Her eyes scanned the rest of the club, but she couldn't spot any of her crowd, so she pushed her way past the other club goers and headed for the exit. She nearly felt like crying when she got outside. She still felt how damp she was between her legs and felt the twitch of excitement that had ached for a hard cock for a split second.

She took out a cigarette she'd made earlier, then walked on, trying to find her lighter. Her hand was shaking as she tried to light her fag, an icy wind attacking her body. She saw an alleyway to her right and headed down it. She stood in the half light that one of the street lights allowed. She lit her cigarette and took a shaky lungful, but then felt a little sick. She stubbed it out as she heard footsteps coming towards her.

'Sarah, I wondered where you ran off to.'

She looked up, her stomach twisting as she

recognised Paul's voice.

'Please, Paul, please stay away from me.'

He came towards her and stood close by. She looked away from him as he said, 'Why? You were getting wet in there. You were enjoying it. I want to be deep inside you. I want to feel your wetness around my cock.'

'Don't,' she said, feeling the ache of excitement between her legs.

'Come on, just be a bit naughty.'

'I can't. It's wrong.' She turned around, but felt Paul's hands grab her arse and pull her back towards him. He wrapped his arms round her and pushed himself into her. She felt his stiffness through his jeans, pressing himself harder against her. 'Can't you feel how horny you make me? I've got to have you.'

'Get off.' She tried to get him off, but he forced her to the wall, pressed her against it. Her face was cold as her cheek pressed into the brick work. Still she could feel him so hard, and now he'd started pushing himself against her, rubbing a little. He had her trapped, so he easily slipped his hand down between her legs and pulled up her skirt. She struggled again as he sucked and bit gently on her neck, his other hand grasping her arse. His weight kept her trapped as he slid his hand between her legs and felt her dripping wet pussy through her tights.

'I want to hear you say you want me to fuck you in every hole you've got,' he whispered in her ear.

'I can't...please don't...'

He found her clit and pinched it gently, then caressed it. She shuddered as his cock pressed against her back.

'You're going to beg for my cock.'

'No...I won't...'

He suddenly grasped her hair and pulled, yanked her head back. 'You will beg for my cock.'

Then she heard his jeans open, and his hand was suddenly on hers, dragging it back towards his fly. Her hand flinched when she felt the hard warmth of his bulging, straining cock.

'Grab it!' he ordered.

She figured she could wank him off and be done with it, so grasped tightly round his pulsating cock. He was so hard. She began to pull him, yanking him slowly as she found his fingers working her clit. Then his other hand slid up to her arse and between her cheeks, and found the tight bud of her anus. He began to tease it while his other hand stroked her clit at the same time. Sarah kept working his shaft, feeling it beating against her palm, the electricity rising up from her soaking wet pussy and her other hole. Suddenly he bent her over, and she leaned against the wall. He was on his knees, tonguing her tight hole, and fingering her pussy, sticking three fingers inside her. She wanted to cum now, and found herself teetering on the edge of an orgasm. She kept pulling herself back from it, telling herself it was wrong, but the guilt seemed to be washing away as her desire was rising.

Then he was up again and yanking up her skirt, pushing her over. She supported herself against the wall as he pushed his cock against her moist slit. It slipped and slid over her moist opening as he tried to thrust into her.

'No, Paul, I can't...' she said and tried to get away, but he grabbed hold of her hair and pulled it, making her yelp.

He pushed his erection into her slit, and she felt it open for him, becoming even more wet. He pushed his hips against her, thrusting himself deep inside. She was filled up with him, feeling the head of his cock straining and throbbing.

'Please, Paul, this is wrong, I can't...'

He pulled himself halfway out and then hammered hard into her again and suddenly bit her shoulder. She shivered with pleasure as he began to suck her shoulder, then biting a little. 'Can you feel my cock inside you, Sarah?'

She didn't say anything, just whimpered and bit her lip. A cry of pleasure was building in her throat, but she quelled it. She couldn't let herself give in and allow her orgasm to be released. Then his free hand tore at her tights and made a hole in them, allowing his fingers to find her anus. He ran his fingers over it as he pounded into her wetness, then licked his own fingers. His wet digits slid into her tighter hole and she nearly buckled. He held her up and shoved himself in her, his fingers deep into her arse. Then he pulled them out and she found suddenly both his hands ripping open her blouse and pulling at her bra. He slid the straps down and allowed her rock hard nipples to be released. As he fucked her hard, he ran his palms over her nipples, then began pinching them gently between his fingers. The electricity seemed to race from her pussy and right up to her breasts, bringing with it a massive wave of excitement. 'You're so fucking wet,' he whispered in her ear, then gently bit on the left lobe. 'Tell me you want to put my cock in all your holes.'

She managed to pull her senses back into focus. 'I can't...Paul, get off me...'

'Tell me, say you want my cock in your mouth...'

'I'll say it if you...if you stop...'

'Ok...say it...' He was panting, his cock ramming in and out, feeling as if it might rip through her.

'I wa...' She nearly choked on the words.

'Say it!' He teased her nipples, toyed with her arse.

'I want your...cock in my...mouth.'

'Good. That's better.' He pulled out of her pussy, but kept her pinned. 'Now, remember I've still got the photo of you. So, you better do as I say.'

He'd lied. The bastard had lied. But she knew he would. She wanted it to be over, but she found herself yearning for her orgasm too.

'Turn round! On your knees.'

Sarah, exhausted, her pussy tingling still, knelt down and looked up.

His wet, glistening cock was hard and twitching right in front of her. It was moist with her juices.

'Lick off your juices. I want you to taste yourself on my cock.' When his cock came towards her mouth, she opened and immediately began tonguing at the head of his erection. She licked off her own juices and felt her pussy begin to pulse with pleasure. She was beginning to ache for his cock, desperate to feel his spurts of cum inside her. She was angry at herself and guilty for now giving in. But she began to hungrily feed on his cock, treating it like it was made of chocolate. But it tasted good anyway. It was silky and smooth on her lips and tongue.

'Make yourself come,' he said, and she used her free hand to stroke her pussy until she felt the burning pleasure rising all over her body.

Suddenly the yearning for his cock was too much to bear, and she pulled her mouth from his erection and said, panting, 'Fuck my pussy. I want you in my pussy.'

He smiled and lifted her to her feet, then pushed her against the wall. He lifted up one leg, and got close to her. She felt him slide into her and she moaned loudly, feeling herself blush.

He was pressed hard against her, his mouth on her neck, sucking and biting, kissing, his now pulsating cock thrusting into her faster and faster.

'I want to come inside you,' he rasped into her ear.

'Fuck me. Harder.' She blushed as she heard her own words. He did, he pounded, pushing himself deeper into her as his fingers squeezed between their bodies and found her clit. He expertly worked her wet bud and the rush of euphoria swept over her. His cock throbbed, and twitched and she knew he was about to release. She grabbed his arse and pulled him even deeper as she began to cum, shaking a little as she moaned and cried. His cock violently trembled as she felt the spurt of his cum shooting out and filling her pussy.

Panting, he slipped to his knees and looked up at her. He smiled and she smiled back even though she was embarrassed. He lurched forward suddenly and grasped her legs, pulled them apart and pressed his mouth between her legs and began lapping at her slick opening. She grasped the wall as his tongue took away her juices and his, hungrily, manically. Then his tongue swirled over her clit again, sending a bolt of pleasure right through her core. He put a hand to her pussy, inserting two fingers into gushing hole. And with his thumb he teased her anus. Again her orgasm began to ripple all over her. She didn't fight it, just opened her legs and let him eat away at her. Her pleasure pulsed, and she moaned and said, 'Paul, I'm coming again. Don't stop. Please...make me come.' When she'd come once more, he got to his feet and kissed her on her mouth. She pulled him to her, but he moved away. She watched him turn away and walk down the alleyway and disappear.

On Tuesday morning, she returned to work, her cheeks burning. She felt ashamed, and guilty, but also a little wet at the thought of what he'd made her do.

Paul was sitting in his usual place, his head turned away. She said good morning, but he didn't say a thing back. She was angry now, furious that he had seduced her and now was ignoring her.

As she plotted her revenge, she saw she had a private message from Paul on Twitter: 'Look under the desk.'

She looked up, but he still wasn't looking her way. Her cheeks burned, but, pretending to adjust her boot, she got down under the desk. She looked up and gasped. She felt herself blush. She looked again and saw Paul's swollen cock was staring at her, smooth and shiny. Then his hand grasped his shaft and began working it.

She couldn't stay under there forever, so got up. She could feel the heat on her cheeks and couldn't bring herself to look at him for the next few minutes.

Suddenly she realised it was her break time. She decided to stay where she was, and try and relax at her desk. Then out of the corner of her eye, she saw a figure walking round her desk and heading right for her. Her face burned again as Paul appeared and pulled up a chair next to her.

'Hi, Sarah,' he said, as if nothing had happened.

'Hello, Paul,' she said but looked away. She looked around, but there was nobody near them. They'd all gone for a break or to someone else's desk.

'Nice night out, wasn't it?' he said.

'Yes...' She went quiet.

He moved closer, positioned himself close to the

desk. 'Looks like we're alone.'

'Yes, but someone'll soon come over.'

Her words didn't seem to dissuade him as he began to unbutton his jeans. He slipped his hand into his boxer shorts and started to rub himself. She looked round, scared that someone might be watching. No one seemed to be looking their way. It was a bloody good job, she thought, as her heart began to race. He was crazy, dangerous. When she looked back at him, he had his cock out, his hand wrapped tightly round it, gently pulling it up and down.

'Put it away!' she said, trembling.

'Not until you kiss it,' he whispered.

'No! I can't. Put it away. You'll get fired.'

He smiled. 'I don't care. Come on, kiss it. You better hurry up before someone comes over.'

She looked round and saw people walking around, some sitting at desks. Then she looked at his raging, fleshy cock. The head was quite purple and shining proudly in the light. She'd never seen it in the day.

'Kiss it.'

She looked around again and then quickly pecked the tip. She tasted him and felt the flood gates open between her legs, the memory of Saturday night flashing in front of her eyes.

'No, properly kiss it.'

'I can't.'

'Yes you can.' He slipped his hand up to her head and pushed her towards his now twitching cock. She kissed it gently, then opened her mouth a little and used her tongue as she would when French kissing. A shiny drop of precum appeared and she licked it away. She felt him stiffen, the blood pumping harder to his erection.

'Suck it, Sarah.'

She gave another look around the room, then put her full lips round the head, feeling it all warm and salty. She sucked, licked, then snogged down the shaft and back up again to the tip. He grabbed her hair and forced his cock deeper into her mouth, then out again and in, fucking her throat. She coughed a little as his cock became even more rigid and pulsated. Then he slipped it out of her mouth and ran the head over her lips, across her face. She tried to put her mouth round it as he moved it around her face. Eventually she fixed her lips around the head and sucked hard and grabbed the shaft and began pulling his erection up and down. She kept jerking him, her heart now vibrating madly, her hands shaking, and her pussy dripping with her juices. At last she felt his cock shudder, then heard Paul groan. He clamped his hand over his own mouth as he let out a deep cry as she felt his ejaculation explode across her tongue. She began to swallow, tasting him and allowing his cum to slip down her throat.

When he let her up, she looked down and saw his cock still twitching and cum oozing a little from the end. She bent down and kissed the rest off his head and smiled.

'You're very good, Sarah,' he said, and kissed and bit gently into her neck. As he got up, he squeezed her bum, then put himself away and walked back to his desk.

She could only watch him walk away, seeing the bulge in his trousers growing again. She felt down between her legs and found her leggings were sodden. It warmed her, the thought of him coming in her mouth, his tongue and fingers on her pussy. She picked up her phone and started to write a private message to Paul: 'I can't believe you did that to me. You abused me. I won't ever let you near me again.

You'll never get to put your hard cock in me again and fuck me and make me cum. You can try and seduce me, but I'll fight back. ;-) xx.'

She blushed as she sent the message and looked guiltily around the room.

When she made sure no one was looking, she touched her clit gently and imagined it was his hand...

THE BOSS OF HER

It had been nearly two weeks since my steamy, quite frankly filthy encounter with my boss, Ella and her best friend. It had stayed with me, sending pulses of pleasure through me as I recalled all the things we had done. But since that night, I had heard nothing from her. Even at work, she had been distant, returning to her professional self.

What had I done? Had I disappointed her? We had both agreed that no one would ever learn what we had done, that it would be our naughty secret, but no more had been said about doing it again.

Was it over?

When I returned to work, sitting in my cubicle, watching her go by, I was deflated. To make matters worse, her outfits had become almost unbearable. She had started wearing shorter, pencil skirts, sheer black or flesh colour tights, showing off her long shapely legs in her high heels. She smelled wonderful, looked amazing. It was as if she was teasing me, flaunting the attraction I had. What was her game?

I kept walking past her office, hoping she'd come out and I could pretend to bump into her. But she never did.

Sometimes I'd pass her in the corridor and she

would be talking to another male employee, laughing at his jokes. Was it done to mess with my mind?

Then a couple of days later, she called me into her office for an evaluation meeting. I had recently been put in charge of a team. We weren't performing very well, but my mind had been else where.

But at last, my boss, my sexual obsession was meeting with me.

She took me through to a large office within our bigger office. There was no one in there but us, so we sat at the centre, facing each other. She was wearing a short grey skirt, very sheer black tights, a tight fitting white shirt, her cleavage tantalising me. She must have known what she was doing.

As soon as I sat opposite her, she crossed her legs. The beautifully erotic sound of the nylon rubbing against nylon filled my ears, making me burn all over.

She looked down at her notes as she said, 'Your little team hasn't been performing very well the last couple of weeks.'

She looked up, staring me in the eyes. 'Why do you think that is?'

I was frozen for a moment, sad that her professional manner was back in place. I cleared my throat. 'It's early days. We've only just...'

'But you knew what you were dealing with.' She uncrossed her legs, then crossed them again. I ached.

My eyes stared down at her legs, the shape of them, her sharp knees, her shapely calves, her heels.

'Are you distracted?' she asked.

'No. Sorry.'

'I think the problem is that you haven't shown leadership, haven't taken charge.'

I looked up into her eyes. 'Well, I feel like a leader should show...'

'Someone in charge, should show they're in charge. They need to do whatever it takes to get the job done.'

One her eyebrows arched as she crossed her legs again, slowly, deliberately, I felt.

'Anything?' I asked, feeling like we were talking about something separate from work.

'Anything goes,' she said, staring into my eyes.

I looked round the room, my eyes fixing on the small glass window of the door, where if someone passed by, they would be able to see us both.

Then her hand, her nails, painted a dark red, caressed her legs, up and down. The burn began again, igniting my desire, making my cock twitch, yawn and grow.

Anything, she had said. Take charge. Is this what she meant?!

Slowly, nervously, I unzipped my trousers. I got hold of my cock, positioning myself with my back to the door. I got my cock out, stroking it, her eyes on me. She was blank, reacting as if I was merely blowing my nose.

I was now hard, my eyes all over her. My cock was wet already. It was now or never.

'Crawl over here and suck my cock,' I said.

'No.' She stared me in the eyes.

'Suck it! Get on your fucking knees and crawl to my cock and suck it!' I trembled, hearing my own words and their commanding tone.

Then she was getting down, kneeling, then crawling, her red lips parting. I held it out to her. Her face reached my cock, but stopped.

'Suck it, kiss it,' I commanded.

'You'll have to make me.'

I put my hand on the back of her head, digging my fingers in her hair, forcing her head to my cock.

100

Her mouth, all warm and wet, wrapped around my cock. I moved her head, pushing it up and down on my now incredibly stiff erection. Oh God, her mouth was sucking me, kissing my cock, her tongue working it's magic. I looked down and her eyes were on me, staring up at me.

I undid my shirt, pulling her hands to my chest, making her tease my nipples. I didn't care anymore, didn't give a shit about who might walk in. I just wanted her mouth round my cock.

I took my cock from her mouth, then rubbed it around her face a little, then caressed it over her red lips. Her lipstick was around my cock, smeared all over it.

'Get up,' I found myself commanding her.

She did as she was told. Then I saw a desk by the far end of the room.

'Go over there and bend over the desk,' I said.

She walked over, bent over it, hands on the corner of the desk, waiting. I walked over, staring at her nice, tight bum in her office skirt. I pulled it up, revealing that she was not wearing any underwear under her tights. I smiled, burning all over. I ran my hands up her legs, over her arse, feeling her quiver a little.

Then I pulled my hand back, then swiped the air and slapped my palm hard against her arse cheek.

She let out a moan.

'Who's the boss?' I asked.

'Me,' she said.

I pulled my hand back further, then slapped her arse harder.

Another deep moan.

'Who's the fucking boss?' I demanded to know.

'Me.'

I grabbed her head back, then slapped her arse

again. 'Who's the fucking boss?'

'You are,' she said. 'You're the boss.'

'What do you call me?'

'Sir.'

'That's right.' My cock was now utterly hard, shimmering with precum. I moved closer, pressing my cock to her arse cheeks, making her let out a little moan.

'I'm the boss. You do as I say. Anything I say.'

'Yes, sir.' She looked round, licking her lips.

My cock twitched. 'Show me your pussy and your arse.'

She leaned face down on the desk, then reached round to her arse, and pulled her cheeks apart, showing everything through her tights. I ran my hands up her legs, cupping her tight hole and her wet pussy. Her tights were wet. I knelt down, began licking her arse and pussy through the tights, making her moan and writhe. Then my mind was working overtime, trying to think of what I could get her to do.

'You have to do anything I say,' I said.

'Yes, sir.'

I looked round the room, remembering that there was a guy who worked in accounts down the corridor. I knew some of the ladies in the office fancied him. He was single. I smiled.

'Come with me,' I said, and took her through the other door, then along the corridor. I looked round at her, but she was just looking at me, a look in her eye that told me she was turned on, a little scared but very aroused.

I looked into his office and saw he was in there, working away.

I turned to Ella. 'Go in there and suck his cock.'

'I won't do that.'

'You have to do what I say. Do it now! Suck his fucking cock.'

'Yes, sir,' she said, then went into his office. I watched through the window in the door. She went in. He greeted her, but she didn't reply, just walked around his desk, knelt down and started unbuttoning his flies.

'What are you...' he started to say, but she grabbed hold of his flaccid cock and started stroking it. He let out a groan of pleasure as it grew hard, then stared down at her as she lowered her head, taking him in her mouth. She started sucking him like her life depended on it. He rested his head back, panting and moaning.

'Oh fuck,' I heard him say.

I was getting hard watching, but a little jealous too. My cock was back in my trousers, but was hard, so I reached in, grabbing it, and started stroking it. She was taking him deep into her mouth, her throat. He was groaning, staring down at her, unable to believe his luck.

'Come in my mouth,' I heard her mumble.

A few seconds later, he let out a moan of pleasure and must have shot his cum into her mouth. She got up, wiped her mouth, and walked out, joining me in the corridor.

'How did he taste?' I asked.

'Not as good as you, sir,' she said.

'Come with me,' I said, feeling my cock grow even harder.

I took her into the men's toilet, making sure it was empty. We went into a cubicle and I ordered her onto her knees.

'Yes, sir,' she said, then knelt down.

I got my cock out, wanking it a little, then rubbing it over her face. 'Suck it,' I ordered and she went to work, hungrily sucking and kissing my cock. First of all, she sucked and kissed the tip, staring up at me all the time, moaning, panting, enjoying it as she gave me pleasure. I reached down and undid her shirt, then pulled down her bra so I could see her nice, quite small breasts. I teased her nipples, pinched them lightly, making her moan even more.

'Get up,' I ordered. 'Turn round.'

She did, so I pushed her against the door. She let out a moan as I pulled up her skirt, revealing her tight little arse in her tights. I squeezed her arse as I kissed her neck and bit her ear.

'I'm going to fuck you,' I whispered into her ear. 'I'll make you my sex slave...'

I grabbed her, putting my hand between her legs, gripping her pussy and her anus, smearing her juices all over her tights. Then I grabbed the gusset and tore at it, ripping her pussy and arse free. I pressed my swollen member against her warm arse cheeks, forcing it further until it was pressed against the tight little bud of her arse. I smeared her wetness over her tight hole, then pushed the tip of my cock into it, pressing, forcing it, until it slowly, all oiled with her wetness, it went into her arse.

'Oh fuck...' she moaned, turning her mouth to me. I reached forward, kissing her mouth, tonguing her as I pushed my cock deeper into her arse, then out, then back in, deeper. I reached round, opening her shirt, getting her small breasts out. I squeezed my hands over them, feeling her nipples hardening at the touch of my palms.

'Who's your fucking boss?' I asked, ramming my cock deeper into her arse.

'You...you are, sir,' she said, half moaning, almost letting out a scream.

My cock was twitching, throbbing deep in her. I started to fuck her harder, squeezing her breasts, biting her shoulder. 'You're mine now. I'm your master.'

'Yes, sir. Yes, master. I'm yours.'

I couldn't hold it in anymore. I started coming, moaning as I pushed in and out, spurting my cum deep inside her tight hole. She groaned, pushing her arse back at me, milking every last drop of cum from me.

Eventually I moved back, pulling myself out of her and letting her get dressed again.

'What's next, sir?' she asked, raising her eyebrows. 'I want to do everything you want.'

'Anything?' I asked, unsure of what I could get her to do. What did I want?

'Anything. I'll do anything you want.' She smiled. 'Even if I don't like it.'

'OK. Come to my place tonight and I'll have something terrible in place.'

She smiled. 'Good. I'll be there at eight.'

What the hell was I going to get her to do? I racked my mind to think what I would want to do to her? Then I thought of bondage. I knew there was a sex shop in town, so slipped in there after work and bought several toys, and handcuffs, and nipple clamps. Then I went home and sat down, thinking.

Then it came to me. I thought of my friend, Dave. He had always been into BDSM, all that kind of thing, along with his wife, a very goth kind of girl who called herself Raven. I smiled to himself as he thought of Raven, her jet black hair, her white skin, her dark red nails, and her shapely figure. I had a secret crush on her too, but of course I had never acted on it.

I decided to call Dave to see if there was any chance he was free this evening.

'Hey, Dave,' I said, when my friend answered. 'How are you?'

'Wow, Mike, haven't talked to you in a while. I'm good. Works OK.'

Dave ran his own business from home, web designing.

'How's Raven?' Dave asked.

'She's good. You still single?'

I laughed. 'Well, funny you should mention that. I've got kind of a date thing tonight. Sort of. Sort of role playing. I've got this sexy boss...'

'You've been fucking your boss? You lucky bastard.'

'I know. Well, listen, any chance you two might want to get in on the action?'

Dave was quiet for the moment. 'Really? What a bit of session? All four of us?'

'Do you think Raven would be up for it?'

Dave let out a laugh. 'Have you met her? She's up for anything. I'll tell her in a bit. She'll love it. Tonight then? When should we be there?'

'Eight. I'll see you then?'

'Oh, yes, we'll be there.'

I buzzed with excitement for the rest of the day, my mind racing, all kind of scenarios shooting through my head. Raven and Ella together. I smiled, my cock twitching at the thought. I wasn't sure what Ella would make of Dave. He wasn't the best looking guy in the world, but he seemed to have a way with the Rock chicks he met. He was big, brutal, sort of, with shoulder length hair.

The time went by slowly. I got dressed, more

casually, in a T-shirt and jeans.

When Ella turned up, she was wearing a tight, and very short red skirt, sheer black tights and black high heeled boots. She had a black off the shoulder top. Her hair was up. She looked stunning, and the sight of her made me throb with excitement.

'So, what have you got planned for me, sir?' she asked as I passed her a glass of wine in my lounge.

'It'll be a surprise,' I said and smiled, sipping my wine.

Ella sat down and crossed her legs. The skirt rode up, so I could see all of her lovely legs. I could also tell she wasn't wearing any underwear again.

'So, you'll do anything I ask?' I said, my cock starting to grow. I touched her face, and she kissed my hand.

'Anything. No questions, no excuses. Sir.'

I ached. I ran my thumb over her lips, then pushed it into her mouth. She sucked on my thumb, hungrily, her eyes staring up at me.

The doorbell rang, so I answered it. When I opened the door, Dave stood there in a black shirt, black jeans. I had forgottem how big he was, how meaty. I'd never seen his cock, but had heard it was long and thick. Another reason the ladies were drawn to him.

Raven was behind him, wearing a black and red basque that squeezed in her milky white cleavage, making it even more beautiful. She had on a short skirt, fishnet tights and boots. My cock grew again. It was going to be a wild night.

'Hey, are we early?' Dave asked, following me back up to my front room.

'No, right on time.' I took them in where Ella was sat on the sofa, her legs crossed. She took them all in, smiling a little.

'Hey,' Dave said to Ella and Mike saw his eyes light up and run all over her body.

'I'm here to be used,' Ella said and stood up. 'I'll do anything Mike wants. Tonight he's my master.'

'Sounds sexy,' Raven said, her eyes finding me with a smile.

'Where do we start?' Dave asked me.

I looked at Ella, then went and fetched the handcuffs I had bought. Ella watched me as I walked round her. 'Put your hands behind your back,' I ordered.

'Yes, sir,' she said, and I clamped them shut.

I looked at Dave. 'Why don't you say hello, Dave?'

Dave smiled then walked over to her, looking her over. He reached out his meaty hand, then ran it over her arms, her shoulders, then her face.

'I'm Dave,' he said. 'I'm going to fuck you.'

She didn't say anything, just nodded.

'Kneel down,' Dave said, putting a hand on her head. She did as she was ordered. Dave undid his trousers, getting his flaccid cock out. My eyes bulged at the size of it, even though it was hardly erect. Dave started to work it, making it stiff. It was a monster.

Then he was taking it to Ella's mouth, directing it to her lips. He clamped a hand over her head, bringing her closer. She opened her mouth wide, taking the huge head of his cock into her mouth with a moan. He forced it in further, making her gag. I could only watch on, jealously suddenly filing me up as Ella began to suck and lick the end of the huge cock. I could hear her moans as she tried harder to take the large member into her mouth.

'What do we do now?'

I realised Raven was addressing me, and turned to look at her. Her full lips were painted dark red, her long dark hair framing her beautifully pale face. My eyes drifted down to her quite large white cleavage. My cock woke up, aching a little at the sight of her.

'I don't know,' I said.

She smiled, then stepped closer to me, her hand reaching out, then pressing against my stiffening cock. 'I think you have an idea.'

She wrapped her fingers around my bulge and squeezed. I let out a sigh, then put my hand on her shoulder, then smoothed it over her left breast. She smiled, then readjusted her basque, letting her very pink nipples poke over the top. I leaned in, taking hold of her left breast, squeezing it, bringing her nipple to my mouth. I ran my tongue over it, then sucked it a little bit, making my cock grow stiff in her hand as I heard her moan.

'We should've done this sooner,' she said, then unzipped me and got my cock out. She took me to the other sofa, made me sick back, then sat a stride me, pushing her breasts in my face. I grabbed them, teasing her nipples, feeling her grind herself over my cock. My eyes drifted up as I kissed and bit Raven's shoulder, watching Ella still sucking Dave's mighty cock, while she moaned with pleasure.

Then Dave had her up, and was making her turn round. He bent her over, pulling up her skirt, then rubbing his hand over her arse and pussy. He tore her tights, then pressed his massive cock to her arse. He grabbed her hair, and started pushing his cock at her wet pussy. I watched, filled with pleasure from Raven's grinding and jealousy at what I was witnessing. What had I done? But it was too late now and it sounded like Ella was enjoying herself.

Raven got down on her knees, then brought my cock to her chest, slipping it between her breasts, still stroking my shaft. Her mouth moved down, kissing and sucking the tip. I looked down, watching her dark red lips sucking my cock. I swelled, remembering all the times I'd fantasised about this moment. Suddenly I felt my orgasm building, ready to let go and cum in her mouth, or better still, over her mouth. No, I wanted it all to last. I tried to control my desire.

Then we both her heard it.

Ella was moaning, almost screaming, saying, 'Oh, fuck, yes, fuck me...harder. Fuck...fuck me with your big cock!'

Raven sat up, turning to see what was going on.

'I've got to get in on this,' she said, then got up and sat by Ella as she was pumped hard. Raven stared into Ella's eyes, then leaned in, opening her mouth, darting out her pierced tongue. Ella did the same, and they started kissing, passionately, wildly. I could hardly take it, watching my boss being hammered by my friend's giant cock and seduced by another woman. I sat back, helplessly, my cock more rigid than ever. I took my cock and stroked it, watching, staring in amazement as my boss was being fucked one end and kissed and seduced at the other.

Ella was now kissing one of Raven's milky white breasts, while her right hand teased her other nipple. Dave was fucking her hard now, pounding, making Ella jerk forward and let out grunts and moans.

'Oh shit,' Ella suddenly said. 'I'm going to cum!'

Raven moved then, slipping her hand between Ella legs, seeming to find her clit and tease it while Dave fucked her faster and faster.

'Oh God!' Ella screamed. 'I'm cuming! Oh fuck!'

Then she lay there, breathing hard, Dave still pumping her, slowly, grunting himself.

'You going to join the action, Mike?' Dave asked over his shoulder.

I was still rock hard, so got up and came over. Dave had his big solid cock in her pussy, that was glistening wet with her juices. Her tight hole was free. I smiled as I fetched some lube, then oiled up her puckered little hole. Ella writhed a little.

'I don't know if I can take...' Ella began to say, but I didn't listen.

'You said anything goes,' I said, pushing my lubed up cock into her tight hole.

Ella gritted her teeth, grunting, nearly screaming as I felt my cock begin to slide in. Dave began his fucking again, and I could feel it. I could feel the huge cock rubbing up against mine. The sensation over took me, sending me into a kind of ecstasy as I looked down and saw Raven's beautiful breasts and Ella's incredible body as she was fucked. Raven got up, left, then came back with a huge pink strap on. Ella opened her mouth immediately and let Raven push the big rubber erection between her beautiful lips. The goth started fucking her mouth, seeming to enjoy it herself as she moaned and grunted.

I looked down at my own swollen cock as I fucked her tight little hole. Mine looked small compared to Dave's huge beast. But it all was almost too much to bear, and I felt his cock twitching.

'I'm going to cum!' I announced.

'Me too!' Dave said, pumping harder. 'Let's cum over her face!'

I watch Dave, pumping his cock, pushing Raven out of the way, pointing his member at Ella's face. I pull out too, rushed to her face, seeing her open her mouth, wanting it. I stroked, looking over her body, then at Raven's perfect breasts. Then I was shooting my load, groaning. Dave came too, loads, endlessly it seemed. Both of our cum spurts over Ella's face, making her let out a satisfied sigh. Then she was licking us clean, spinning her head between us, hungrily licking us.

She crawled towards Raven, parting her legs. Raven just relaxed back, nodding, opening her legs. My boss seems to love pussy as much as she loved cock, it seemed, as she went to work, running her tongue over Raven's glisteningly wet opening, her swollen lips, and eventually her erect clit. The goth girl let out moan after moan, nodding her head. 'Yes, yes, baby, oh shit,' Raven said, her own hands grasping her own nipples and teasing them.

We men watched on, hypnotised by the scene, playing with our cocks, getting ourselves ready, enjoying the show. It isn't long before Dave's shoving his huge cock in Raven's face, pushing it into her mouth, muffling her moans. I take a look at Ella, at her beautiful arse and pussy. Bit by bit my cock starts to rage again, swelling as I watch the scene. I grab Ella's arse, parting her cheeks, then push myself into opening, feeling her oily wet lips welcome me in. She's already moaning, so it's hard to tell if my cock is doing its job, so I carry on fucking her, hard, pushing in, pulling out, griping her hips.

I look up, see Ella's head buried deep in Raven's pussy. But then I realise it's not just her clit that's getting the attention. She's running her tongue from her clit right down to her tight little puckered hole, making Raven moan. The moans are muffled, her mouth filled up with Dave's massive member that he's forcing down her throat, practically choking her. His balls touch her chin, her face almost purple. Then he pulled out, and Raven fights for breath, coughs, then grabs his arse and brings his cock in for more. I keep fucking Ella, sinking my fingers into her arse. Then I pulled my hand back and slapped her arse cheek. She quivered and let out a deep grunt. I took it as a good sign, so slapped her harder. She bucked and let out another moan.

'Harder!' she moaned, taking her mouth from Raven's clit.

Then I remembered something I bought from the shop earlier. I came back with the small black paddle and struck her arse with it. She let out a half scream, half moan. I put my cock back inside her, then smacked her arse harder and harder.

'I'm cuming!' she groaned, so I hammered my cock harder, and smacked her arse in time with my thrusts until she was panting and moaning and telling me she was cuming. She came twice, maybe three times before she collapsed to the sofa.

I'm breathing hard, my cock still standing to attention, when Dave goes off and brings back a collar and chain, the kind a dog or gimp might wear. He put the collar round Raven's neck. She immediately gets on all fours and he took her for a walk round the room, smacking her every now and then. It's then I notice the marks across her perfect round, white arse. They look like marks left by a whip or similar. I realised suddenly that their sexual world was much darker and weirder than mine would ever be.

'Come and fuck her,' Dave said to me.

I was still hard, so I went over, getting on my knees, seeing Raven lift her arse towards me. I grew hard at the sight of both her pink openings. I choose her tighter one first, and pushed my cock in. She welcomed me quite easily, with a subtle gasp. I started fucking, grasping hold of Raven's hair. I was ready to fire my cum inside her within seconds, but I held out. I looked round to see Dave pulling Ella up from the sofa, then turning her around to face him and kissing her, his hands all over her breasts, squeezing them, pinching her nipples. She kissed him, hungrily, then sank back when he began to suck her nipples and cup her pussy. She moaned, then laid back, spreading her legs as Dave put his mouth to her lips and clit. The jealously pounded in me as I fucked Raven harder, the anger pulsating in my brain. Was it he that she now lusted after? Don't get me wrong, I didn't have feelings for her, apart from desire and want. After all, she was married and I didn't want to come between them. But sexually I wanted to make her mine.

'Oh fuck, fuck me harder!' Raven shouted, half moaning, looking at me over her shoulder.

So I did, digging my fingers into her hips, her arse, directing my cock upwards, rubbing it against her g-spot. I fingered her arse, slapped her cheeks until they glowed red, getting out my tension. Raven kept on, pushing back against me, grunting, telling me, begging me to fuck her, to cum inside her. I kept on going, always one eye on Ella and Dave who were now fucking. She was sat over him, her pussy riding his massive cock, her hands all over his massive chest. She was moaning, and cuming by the sounds of it.

'I'm cuming!' Raven groaned, bringing my attention back to her. I kept going, intensifying my fucking, fingering her clit until she came, noisily. She laughed, then laid on the floor and then lit a cigarette.

I turned to see Ella climbing off Dave, the big man breathing hard, his cock shiny and wet, and becoming a little flaccid.

My boss caught my eye and came over.

'What now, boss?' she asked, wrapping her arms around my neck.

I kissed her. 'I'd like to get you on your own and fuck you.'

She smiled. 'You know I'm married, right? You know this can never be anything more than just fucking for pure pleasure...boss.'

I smiled, nodding. 'I know. It's all I want. Now let's get out of here.'

'Is that an order?' She raised her eyebrows.

'Yes. Yes it is.'

Printed in Great Britain
by Amazon

39444767R00067